SOMEWHERE *to* GO

Shambhavi, born and brought up in Lucknow, is an alumnus of Loreto Convent. She has done Bachelors in Computer Applications and post-graduation in Mass Communication.

She is currently persuing her PhD in Mass Communication and Media.

Being a mother of two sons, aged eight and nine, and wife of an IPS officer, she has a good understanding of nature, life and its various dimensions. Writing interests her and makes her feel lighter, enriched and thoughtful. The author can be reached at shambhavitheauthor@gmail.com.

SOMEWHERE

To

GO

SHAMBHAVI

RUPA

Published by
Rupa Publications India Pvt. Ltd 2017
7/16, Ansari Road, Daryaganj
New Delhi 110002
Sales Centres:

Allahabad Bengaluru Chennai
Hyderabad Jaipur Kathmandu
Kolkata Mumbai

ISBN: 978-81-291-4742-4

First impression 2017

10 9 8 7 6 5 4 3 2 1

The moral right of the author has been asserted.

Printed and bound in India by Repro Knowledgecast Limited, Thane

This book is dedicated to
Suruchi, Rajesh,
Samarth and Shivaya

Chapter 1

THUNDERSTORM AND lightning accompanied by heavy rains lashed against the city, and the weather was reason enough for the citizens to wake up with a smile. The social networks were abuzz with everyone sharing pictures, quotes, songs and videos. The rains gave them that rare chance to sit back with a cup of coffee, free their minds and smile looking at the sky, and start the new day afresh.

Amidst the sound of the rain came a beautiful voice, 'Aysher, Aysher, get up! We are already late for office.' The voice was of a girl in her early twenties—fair with black eyes, long hair, tall and attractive. She was Risha, a newsreader, who lived with her boyfriend, Aysher.

Aysher was in his late twenties and a colleague of Risha. Risha's professional senior, he was a resourceful senior correspondent. Aysher's personality could be summed up by saying that he made all the heads turn anywhere he went. He was handsome and complete with piercing eyes, spiked hair, and a beautiful complexion.

Aysher and Risha had been living together for a year now and made quite a perfect couple. They met during her internship with the news channel where they ended up working together a few times. He fell for her innocence and dedication. With some of Aysher's guidance, Risha was now one of the top newsreaders of the channel.

Risha came to Aysher's bedside with two steaming cups of coffee and pleaded him to get up. 'Look at the awesome weather,' she said. Aysher looked out of the window and turned towards Risha. He wasn't always vocal about his affections, but Risha was the essence of his life, someone who brought him some peace in this fast world. He was like the sea that always came roaring towards the shore that was Risha, always calming down by her touch. He knew her to be his rock, and thought it alright to go easy on expressing his feelings. Her eyes looking at the drizzling rain gave him more peace than a long vacation could. 'It's beautiful! Isn't it?' murmured Risha. Aysher picked his cup of coffee and said 'Yup! It indeed is.' After a few seconds Risha said 'Oh my God! It's eight, get up! Get up! The traffic is already a mess. We won't make it to work on time.' 'Calm down, sweetie, let's not worry about these things,' he said while hugging her. A hug from Aysher made her day. What could be a better start!

The rain got heavier as Aysher and Risha started to get ready for office with some loud music playing in the background. It drained out the sound of Aysher's phone. On seeing four missed calls, he called back. 'Good morning, Sir. There is a story for you. The lightning has killed a family of five in the morning today. I am waiting for you with the OB van at the highway crossing,' said the caller. 'Great, I will see you in fifteen minutes,' he replied.

The car sped towards the highway; Risha was touching up on her make-up while Aysher continued being on the phone.

'Search for some points till I reach the site, we need to spice up the story. I will be there in five to ten minutes,' he instructed. Risha put a stop to the make-up and shouted in amazement and disgust, 'How can you talk like this? Five people of a family are dead and you want to spice things up?' He tried explaining, 'It's not so, Risha. I feel the same way as you do, but you know this is my job.' Not satisfied, Risha replied, 'You have forgotten that you are a human being, have a heart! Every unforeseen incident is not a spicy story! Wake up!'

By the time Aysher reached his destination, the car fell silent. Before getting off, he asserted, 'Work is work. This is how the media works and I am a part of it. If I don't sell this news story, someone else will. I am just doing my job. It has not been easy for me to get this far in only three years. Risha, do not forget that you too are part of the same industry and happily enjoy the perks of our jobs. Wake up! Remember, hard work pays, but clever work pays even more. I know I am being rude but this is not a dream, it is reality and it's harsh. Take care. I will see you in the news room.' He rushed towards the OB van which zoomed towards the site of the accident.

Risha sat motionless for a few seconds and then shifted to the driver's seat. She felt like crying as she mechanically drove the car to work. She was going on air in the next half an hour. Aysher had never been so rude before, she felt he had changed a lot in the last few months.

The weather was still the same; the street children danced, young boys zoomed on motorbikes, couples walked hand in hand on the pavement, trees swayed in happiness. The road side stall served steaming tea to its customers. Everyone seemed happy except her.

She reached office and went straight to the news room. The technician said, 'Eight minutes and you go on air.' Risha had so much going on in her head but barely had the time to think about those things. She checked herself in the mirror and wiped out the car incident from her mind. Preparing herself mentally, she said to herself, 'Come on, time to buck up.'

The Risha who sat on the newsreader's seat was not the emotional Risha. She was Risha, the most popular newsreader of the channel. She gave a look at the top stories and found Aysher's story among them.

The countdown began and it went...5, 4, 3, 2 and 1.

'Good morning, this is Risha. The news at this hour...'

It was a long session for Risha; she communicated really well with the audience. No wonder she was the best newsreader the channel had. She worshipped her work and was dedicated towards it. 'Thanks Risha, that was great,' said her director. Risha smiled and went to the office coffee shop.

She sat near the window and stared outside. Slowly she transformed from Risha, the newsreader to Risha, Aysher's girlfriend who had always given hundred percent to her relationship. 'One black coffee, please,' she said to the waiter and continued to look outside.

The wind had softened and it now blew gently. The thundering of the sky had also stopped and it was drizzling. Risha extended her hand and could feel the breeze, the rain, the love, the joy but amidst all this, where is her love? She pulled her hand in and thought she had no right to enjoy the weather and be happy. Her thoughts were interrupted when the waiter said smilingly, 'Your coffee, ma'am.' He placed coffee on the table and asked if she wanted anything else. 'No, thanks,' she said with an artificial smile.

She sipped the coffee and started thinking deep. The darkness of the coffee matched the dark clouds outside, she felt them approaching her life.

Aysher's words haunted her. Has he changed? He said all those bitter things! Every word he said was true, but... He has always been so sweet and calm, he made her feel complete. What has changed him? It seemed he didn't love her the way he used to.

Her thoughts were suddenly interrupted by a voice, 'This is for you, Ma'am.' It was a small chocolate cake with 'Sorry' written on it with icing. She lifted her face to look at the waiter but saw Aysher standing in front of her.

He was drenched—under the pink formal shirt clinging to his body, one could see his fair skin clearly. Small droplets were dripping from his hair. He was smiling and had twinkle in his eyes. He had flowers in one hand and balloons in the other, and obviously became the centre of attraction. Risha looked down at the cake and turned her face to look outside the window. People around eagerly watched them.

Risha could not behave like this with Aysher. She looked back into his eyes and her heart lit up with joy. Her heart beat faster, she was excited that her love is back. She said nothing and smilingly extended her hand for the flowers and the balloons. She changed the order—two espresso this time.

Aysher initiated the conversation, 'Try the cake Risha, it is from your favourite bakery. Nice weather! I hope you like the balloons and the flowers.' As things were getting normal between them, the people inside the coffee shop focused on their work now. Risha took a deep breath and said, 'Don't try to deviate from what happened between us. I believe in sorting things out and instead of burying them unsorted. Else they get so complicated that there remains no way of solving them. Aysher, what is the matter? This is not the first day you are behaving like this. I am not able to take it. Please help me, so that I can help you.'

These sincere and true words from Risha made him emotional and he responded, 'I know something is not going right.' Aysher wanted to continue, but was interrupted by the waiter who came with their order. After he was gone, Risha said, 'Can we go to some other place?' This idea was welcomed by Aysher. Both smiled at each other, picked up their belongings, and went out of the coffee shop, and out of the office.

It was still raining, they headed towards their favourite destination: the Delhi-Chandigarh highway. It is always a treat to have a meal at the dhaba, with great food, loud music and company of friends. But they needed some time alone today, so they kept sitting inside the car.

As they parked, a young boy knocked on the window and asked, 'Order, sahib?' Two ginger teas and samosas were ordered and the boy hurried back to his kitchen to fetch it. The samosas and the steaming tea were served in no time. This was the place they often hung out with friends and shared tea over gossip and discussions over career, films, songs, silly jokes and food. But today, it was a bit different.

On their way to the dhaba, both of them refrained from continuing the discussion. After the order, Risha, who could not hold back, initiated, 'Aysher, I think you want to say something.' He started with denying, 'Me? No way, did I say something?'

Risha, got frustrated, said, 'Don't test my patience. I did not come all this way to listen to your jokes. If you have something serious to share, do so. Otherwise I can go home on my own. The whole time I was under the impression that you wanted to speak to me.' A tear trickled down her cheek. She was an intelligent, smart, educated and helpful, but a very emotional, person.

Aysher had a different personality. He could say things very easily but this one seemed difficult. His heart felt heavy, something was pinching him continuously, but he suppressed his feelings. Finally, he spoke very softly, 'Do you feel cheated by me?' and paused. 'Unwillingly, when I am at work, I change into a totally different person. It is opposite to my basic nature, but my profession demands that from me. I joined the media to do something directly for the people, something that would bring their problems to focus. It's about raising a voice for people who are deprived of their basic rights. It's about bringing justice to their lives. Service to mankind in a very small way was my desire, but the situations around do not allow me to work in that direction.'

Aysher sipped his tea, totally submerged in his thoughts, and continued, 'When I first joined the news channel, I got stories that were true. No one even bothered to glance at those stories. They were regarded useless even though they were all true. Sometimes I even risked my life to get them, but all efforts turned futile. The stories were thrown on my face, and I was considered good for nothing. Some even made fun of me behind my back.'

His face became red as these unpleasant memories were being revived. Confessions are always difficult. Aysher paused for some time, looked outside the window, and continued. 'When you first met me, I had learnt the so-called ways of the media industry. It's a race at the end of the day, and if I would not have changed, I would not have survived. The change was not easy, but I had no choice.'

'Then I started to collect stories that would appeal to masses, and the news channel. I learnt all the ways of getting my work done by hook or by crook. I did sting operations as per the demands of the channel. I earned myself a name and a position. I made contacts in each and every field, so that no story could slip from my hand and my channel could have the first breaking news. Now you can see by yourself, every time I get a phone call, I get a new story. It wasn't easy; I sweated under the sun, got drenched in the rain and shivered in the cold, to get myself a story. Only so that I could survive in this industry.'

'You think I like to add spice to the story. I don't. But I have to manipulate the truth. No one wants to know the truth. Not even the public. Truth is too hard to listen and digest, taking it in is not easy. Sometimes, I have to save people whom I know, sometimes their friends or relatives, and sometimes someone in the media asks me to modulate the story. Just a word here and there, and the whole meaning changes. It's not that the whole lot of people working in the media are like me. There are some who did not change their rules, they are also recognized but, it took a lot of time. I could not wait and needed a quick career boost.'

'Each story that I do, I kill some part of the truth behind it. In return, the killed truth kills me like slow poison. I do not like talking about it. I am getting depressed and unsatisfied, day by day. No one can help me because I am the reason, my life is a total waste...I think so.'

All this while, Risha was listening in attention. It was difficult for her to believe that Aysher was so broken from inside, the situation is way more tense than she had thought. She kept her glass of tea aside and held Aysher's hand tightly. In a soft voice she said, 'Don't say so Aysher, I am your support. You can rely on me. I know that you are giving a lot to the industry but you cannot let it weigh you down. We are just puppets…mere puppets. It's not your fault.'

Men don't usually cry but their expressions say it all. Aysher seemed like a prisoner of his situation. He clinched his steering wheel tightly and said in frustration, 'What do I do to reduce my sins? How do I punish myself? The whole situation, and things around, will not let me change for the better.'

All was quiet after that. Only the sound of the rain could be heard. Chotu, the small boy at the dhaba broke the silence, 'Anything else?' Aysher gave him a hundred rupee note, and said, 'the bill and the rest is for you.' The boy got very happy and ran towards the dhaba with a wide smile.

Risha was used to Aysher's acts of kindness; distributing toys and sweets to the children on the streets, to kids in orphanages, but she was completely unaware of the pain and dissatisfaction that lay hidden under his image of always being Mr Cool. He made friends very easily and made everyone comfortable in his presence, but who could bring him to peace? This was like the moon wanting to borrow some light from the sun. But she was not his sun, for sure.

Risha felt satisfied as she had been a good listener to Aysher, and promised herself that she would do something to help him, and as an extension, help herself and their relationship.

Both said nothing and felt each other's presence. They drove back to the crowd of the city. Man is a social animal and passes all stages in the society, which he makes and which, in turn, make him. They both cannot do without each other and also have a lot of differences. Sometimes there is so much of confusion that one cannot listen even to his heart.

Chapter 2

$\mathcal{J}$HE NEXT day both of them felt lighter, as they understood that the real problem had come to limelight, it could be solved easily. Their cheer and positivity soon got overpowered by work. Both had only one thing in mind—work, work and only work.

The following month was the busiest month for the whole country, and media industry had no time even to breathe—the dates of the Lok Sabha elections were announced. Every event, every happening, was newsworthy and capable of influencing voters. Everything had to be covered.

The code of conduct was announced. The Election Commission, along with its officials, was working day in and day out for the smooth functioning of the elections. The politicians had to keep a low profile and everyone was canvassing in different parts of the country. Each statement could make a difference.

Aysher, being one of the most hardworking, dedicated, knowledgeable and resourceful journalists, was asked to cover the important incidents. Due to his workaholic nature, he forgot about his state of mind, kept his feelings inside and prioritised his work.

He was sent to different parts of the country and before he

could finish at one place, he was instructed to go somewhere else.

His efficiency as a worker was becoming a curse for him. He was given tough assignments and was simply told that he was the best and this was a time to prove himself. When he joined, he wished that a day would come when his hands will be full of assignments, and when he was finally living that reality, he was not happy. Desires change and so do situations; when his wish finally got fulfilled, he wanted something else.

He was being utilised by the channel. He knew that when the elections would get over, he would not be promoted easily unless he pulled all the known ropes.

Risha also had no time. She was busy in the newsroom 24×7. It was becoming difficult for her to hide her dark circles due to lack of sleep and being overworked. She didn't have the time to call Aysher, nor did he. Meeting each other in their apartment also became occasional, as their time slots were always clashing with the another's. If they met, they would just discuss about work.

Aysher's temporary home became the OB van in which he used to travel for stories. His refreshment was tea and biscuits that were served by the roadside. Sometimes Risha sent him home-made food. When Aysher started living with her, he just liked Risha but slowly he started loving her. She taught him how to live for your partner.

Risha had always been there for him but he had taken her lightly. She was dedicated to him—from putting the towel in the bathroom or taking out his clothes for the day, and yet, she had never demanded anything from him. All she asked for was being with him all her life. Her ideal time was when she used to listen to Aysher talk for hours, but Aysher never asked Risha if she would like to say something and if he could lend his ears.

Risha went against her own ideals when she decided to accept Aysher's suggestion of living together. She was indeed a modern girl but her heart was seeped in the morals of the Indian culture, she was deeply attached to the roots. A live-in relationship was against her principles but she accepted it as Aysher did not want to marry and get committed. Risha's parents were not in favour of this step. They initially even stopped talking to her, but then later bowed down to her decision. This was the biggest step she had taken in her relationship; she'd always give it everything she could to make it work.

Aysher sometimes got irritated of her love towards him. He used to test her and check her patience. It was not that Aysher was not a good person, but his priority was work and not Risha, and for Risha, Aysher was everything.

Once the elections came to an end and the results were announced, they planned a holiday with friends. Risha knew the stress both she and Aysher were in but her love made her more concerned for him than her own self. She did want some quality time with him, to take their relationship a step forward. She wanted to talk about marriage and that would require for both of them to be in a relaxed atmosphere.

They were a small group of friends which consisted of six couples; some friends and their partners. They had started from Delhi at night and had planned to reach Pithoragarh by the next evening.

The journey was relaxing for all, they had taken a break after a long time. Spending quality time with friends was the best stress buster. They enjoyed the road-side food, caught up on their sleep, listened to songs, clicked pictures, laughed at silly jokes, made fun of each other, discussed office, gossip and politics. This was fun, real fun.

Aysher enjoyed each moment and caught up on his sleep. On waking up in the bus, he saw that everyone else was asleep, even Risha. He chatted with their driver and found out that it would take them another forty-five minutes to reach their breakfast stop. He tried going back to sleep but couldn't, he then tried to work on his laptop but soon got bored. He began looking outside the window.

The bus was at the speed of seventy and Aysher saw it slowly leaving things behind; the trees, the houses, the people—everything was left behind and only the sun stood still.

The sound of the highway traffic was background music, as the wheels moved and made him aware how much they were like his life. The control of the wheels was with the driver, the wheels had no right to think about themselves; his life was the same. It went round and round, always and continuously. But soon something struck him, he is not a wheel? The creator has given him a mind of his own so that he could make decisions for himself and take full control of his life. 'Who the hell is controlling my life? Why have I used it to only run after success? Why didn't I run after happiness, which can even come through small things?' Thud! That was the sound his heart made. What was the reason for this? Why didn't he realize it before? The anchor to one's life is family, which was missing in his case. Parents and siblings are the first people one depends on. Friends these days turn into foes; using people for your own benefit is the mantra for the world today. Yes, Risha was, of course, there for him, but…a lot of questions started crowding his mind. 'What do I want from her?' She was actually the only one Aysher could depend on in this whole world but he rarely shared his feelings with her. It was almost as if she was sharing her life with him, and Aysher was just sharing an apartment. Sometimes, he felt she deserved better. He valued her but seldom made her feel special. For every person he met, he could only think that the person wanted some favour from him. Else, he would think they are all trying impress him. It seemed like he was running but without a destination. Each time he achieved a goal, he made another impossible destination his goal. And each time, the distance between him and the goal kept on increasing. The effort he had to put to reach this goal kept increasing; the number of people he had to use and impress to get there also kept increasing, leaving him unhappy in the end.

Aysher's thoughts were suffocating him; he immediately got up from his place and went to sit beside Risha. He gently touched her hand and the flow of positive energy made him feel much better.

The bus stopped at a small dhaba for some morning snacks, and started again for their destination. Aysher and Risha utilised this time to the fullest. They were like the couples who were destined and fortunate to be with each other. Both were giggling, complaining and teasing each other. It started to get cooler as they reached higher altitudes. The scenic hills, smell of the mountain grass, the dewy grounds lifted everyone's spirits. Aysher took a deep breath and looked at Risha and said, 'Thank you for bringing me here, darling. You are my anchor. I love you and I am blessed to have you by my side.' Risha smiled and hugged him.

The ascent made Risha uneasy and Aysher did his best to

take care of her. They continued to look outside the window and enjoy the beautiful scenery. A light drizzle delayed their commute and they reached their hotel late. By the time they reached the hotel, they were all tired and checked into their respective rooms, and called the day off.

Chapter 3

THERE ARE times when the body becomes its own master and controls its activities. Aysher was extremely tired when he slept, and when the body was a little relaxed, it automatically woke him up. As soon as his eyes opened, he thought that he is late for office and jumped out of the bed. He soon remembered he was in a hotel and on a holiday. No matter how much you sleep, the chance to go back to sleep a second time, is always a prize. With a smile he went back to bed, curled himself in the blanket and gazed out.

Dawn was still an hour away and the birds were still asleep. The drizzle outside continued and he could hear the tapping of the drops. Everything was so silent and calm that one could even count the number of drops. Tap! Tap! Tap! It went on and on... The room also had an unusual smell. Aysher took a deep breath and felt as if he was walking through jungles. His thoughts took him to another world; the smell of grass crushed under his feet combined with the smell of the rain energised him to walk. He was walking alone...all alone in the jungle. Some might think this to be a dangerous thing to do, but he felt no stress, fatigue or anxiety. He kept walking all alone and enjoying every step. The small wild flowers were his guide and the trees his companion. Soon the logical Aysher asked the Aysher walking alone in the jungle, 'Where are you going?' And then the one in the jungle answered, 'nowhere, and wherever my lord wants to take me! When he is my father and capable, I can go anywhere without fearing, he will foresee all and guide me.' As soon as the tapping of the water droplets from the terrace stopped, his thoughts came to a standstill and he came out of the imaginary jungle.

His thoughts shook him. He questioned himself, 'Why am I feeling so strange? Everyone in our society is living the same life. They are inhaling the same competitiveness and exhaling the same crudeness. When God created us, he would not have thought that his best creative work would turn out to be such. Each and every human being knows this, and still they do not make an effort to change, and the excuse is that, they will be crushed if they behave like an angel.' Each one thinks that to survive, one has to fight. Aysher stared at his hands and kept staring at them from that point his mind became blank.

After some time of peaceful blankness, he got up and walked towards the balcony; it was a small balcony sufficient enough for two to stand. He could hardly see anything because of the fog that covered everything. He sat on the little edge that divided the room and the balcony and circled his arms around his legs to keep warm. The fog was slowly moving. He soon remembered something he did as a kid; making shapes out of the clouds. He started using his imagination to give shapes to the fog. When we are alone and there is no one to judge, the pure inner soul gets revealed. After some time, the fog thinned down and soon the beauty uncovered.

Aysher's balcony was facing a small valley with houses

emitting smoke. Small roads went up and down the hill making it a picturesque site no one could resist; it was like a perfect portrait of the almighty. Slowly it became clearer. The gigantic, strong, determined, and welcoming mountains appeared in his view and Aysher kept looking at them. He closed his eyes and tried to feel the beauty around. The sight loosened all his thoughts and as the fog got lightened with the sun, his contemplations became clearer. Only thing visible was the path ahead looking at which gave him immense peace inside.

After a while, a ball of cotton-like rainclouds appeared and it started to drizzle again…Aysher could see people using colourful umbrellas as they traversed the narrow roads. The mountains were opening up new scenes every now and then and in the middle of all this, he could hear the sound of the piano being played. He imagined a small girl playing a piano and the smile on her face now appeared on Aysher's face. The tapping sound on the balcony's roof with the breeze, music, and view made his heart swing. His mind lost all control of his body and it swayed. His eyes were now shining, his smile broadened and he started to tap his feet.

Risha heard the sound of his feet tapping and came out to join Aysher. He had forgotten she was sleeping inside; she hugged him and cheerfully exclaimed, 'You are back, you are back, and I knew this holiday would rejuvenate you. Thank God!' Aysher enjoyed the nature like it was food and he was hungry for years.

Aysher didn't want to hold back and extended his hand towards Risha, and they both danced to the tunes of the rain and the breeze. It was a blissful moment.

He climbed on the chair and spreading both hands, asked

Risha, 'Can you feel what I am feeling? This is life Risha, this is God, and this is Him. This is truth, see it is so captivating. I love it.' Then getting down from the chair and holding the railing of the balcony, he addressed the sky, 'Where are you, God? Please come and guide me as your loving child. I have lost my path, hold my hand.' He raised his hands and closed his eyes, as if reaching out to Him. The rain touched his hands, he could feel each drop, and each seemed to have its own innocent story, and each drop was trying to calm him down. His words reverberated in the valley and echoed with energy and freshness. Aysher had no control over himself, and he continued to talk to God, 'Come, my Lord! Walk with me! Talk with me! I have lost all my energy, please give me strength. I am your lonely child. Show me your love. I love you.'

'And, I love you,' Risha interrupted and held his hand. They sat down on the couch holding each other's hands and she said, 'Aysher, what I said now is not unknown to you. You have heard it a hundred times but this time, it's not the same. This time I want you to respond and express your love like never before.' She paused, and a tear rolled down her cheek and landed on their clasped hands.

'I have gone against every value a woman belonging to a middle-class family needs to adhere to. Our live-in relationship was without the consent of my family. From a crime reporter, I became a newsreader because of you. The society does not see me as your wife but only as your girlfriend, this is not something I want forever in my life.'

She clasped his hands tighter and said, 'Aysher, I am a girl, I cannot go on sacrificing everything in a relationship and get nothing in return. I know you love me as your soul mate but Aysher, the society needs to define a relationship as a confirmation of love. I want to be in a stable relationship with you. I have dreams, which are waiting to be fulfilled. I want my right on your life, as a wife. You love me and I love you but there are things beyond that.' By now her voice had started to tremble, she was feeling helpless having such a candid expression in front of Aysher. When she was in college, she was a bold and strong girl who hated women who did not focus on their career and cried over breakups. Now, she was in the same situation. She wanted to bring about a radical change in the media industry. She was the girl in college who outdid boys in every way. The day she met Aysher for the first time at their workplace, she was smitten. Just like a queen who lays down her armour and waits for her knight in shining armour, she had kept her guards down.

Aysher felt empathetic and said, 'Risha, I understand what you're saying. I should console you but I want to tell you what's really in my mind. I want to be truthful, at least to myself. Dancing to life's every tune has crushed my inner self. I feel shattered. This place gives me immense positivity. My past deeds have left marks on my soul.'

'I want to sit and reassess my life now. I feel sorry for what I have done, and sincerely wish to be forgiven. I want to laugh whole heartedly and make my soul light and free.' To this Risha caringly asked, 'Can I be of any help?' Aysher kindly said, 'Your plan for this holiday is wonderful. You forced me to take a vacation, otherwise I would not have experienced this feeling.'

It started to rain heavily, and they held each other's hands and enjoyed the weather. Risha was feeling lighter after expressing herself and Aysher was entering a thought process that he had never experienced before.

The next day was spent enjoying with friends, chatting around the bonfire, trekking the hill side and dancing. Aysher was enjoying all this, but his mind continued to search for something more. He loved the company, but knew something was amiss. He realized that it was hard to bring happiness to one's self. All the activities brought a smile to his face, but could not touch his heart. Aysher wanted to bring about a drastic change in himself but realized it was difficult to change staying within an old environment. The old manipulative Aysher was still alive in the conversations and memories of his companions. The conflict disturbed him and without informing anyone, he silently slipped out and went for a long walk.

He preferred to walk the route the villagers took. Aysher picked a long wooden stick and cleared his way with it. Walking to nowhere specific in the midst of nature was immensely relaxing. He sat on a big rock and observed the surroundings. The swift breeze caressed him like a mother who has met her son after a long time.

Aysher felt relaxed and realized sometimes the most important thing was to give company to one's self. This little walk opened up all the questions he had been asking himself; he closed his eyes and saw Risha's smiling face. The thought of sharing an entire life with such a person seemed like a blessing. Aysher could feel a force wanting him to go and propose marriage to Risha. It was as if his dark life was being illuminated by Risha's smile and her love. He immediately got up and ran towards the main road with all his energy. He was so engrossed in his thoughts that he didn't realize when he reached the main road. 'Smash!', and all his dreams shattered.

Aysher was run down by a speeding car on the main road. He held to an invisible string of hope as he fell on the ground. The driver of the car used his horns and headlight to avoid the accident and even turned the car the other side to save him. After the accident, the owner of the car came running to see if Aysher was OK and after making sure he was fine, he shouted, 'Are you deaf or blind or both? People like you spoil the life of innocent people like us. Crazy!' Aysher was staring at him. He was speechless and amazed that he was alive. But why did the Almighty save him? For what? To bear more pain? He was lying on the ground like a cloth which had fallen off a clothing line. It was death that came near him but was stopped in the nick of time. By that time, some people had gathered around to help him. They made him sit on the road side and served water. After some time, everyone dispersed and Aysher sat there all alone only with his thoughts as company. He kept sitting there till his friends came searching for him. Seeing bruises on Aysher's body, they got worried and wanted to take him to the doctor. But Aysher convinced them that he was feeling better and just wanted to go to the hotel. On his way, the memories of the encounter with death haunted him.

The basic realities of a man's life are living and dying. After a whole life of manipulating time, coming face to face with death, shook him. He answered the queries of his friends with short sentences before immersing himself in thoughts again. He questioned himself whether he was a child of God or a devil who just knows how to use people for his own benefit. The Almighty made him an orphan so that he could always feel a lack. Maybe it was a lesson for him. And now when he was brought face to face with death, he was given another chance.

As soon as the car stopped outside the hotel, Risha came running and embraced Aysher. She was crying bitterly. Seeing her brimming with emotions, Aysher apologized and proceeded towards their room.

On reaching the room, Risha said, 'Why the hell are you punishing yourself because of me? I am your culprit. From now, I will never talk of marriage and will even go away from your life till you call me back.' By this time she was sobbing uncontrollably, she looked at Aysher and went straight out of the door.

It was a strong hit to his weak mental state, and he didn't know how to react. His life was changing every hour. In a few hours, his girlfriend was walking off the relationship only after hours of wanting to marry him. A few hours earlier, he was unable to understand his own mood swings and when he did understand them and made a decision, he met with an accident. It was turning out to be a jigsaw puzzle with not even one block in place.

Sometimes reactions don't come easily, so he lay down on the sofa and shut his eyes. God obviously had something in mind for Aysher and He was continuously pushing him towards it.

Chapter 4

IT WAS still dark when Aysher sat on a couch by the window side, clasping both his hands tightly to save himself from the cold. The fear of the hazy path ahead was clearly visible on his face.

His past flashed in front of his eyes; his career, social life, friends, colleagues. By the end of it, he still sat there not knowing what to do. All he knew was that this was draining him from inside.

He shut his eyes, and said to himself repeatedly that he was not weak, but strong enough to face any situation. He told himself that it was just a phase that would pass, but as he opened his eyes, he was again lost. He tried to remember an incident that would inspire him but could think of nothing.

Only a dead end seemed to be his destiny. It was like standing on the peak of a mountain and the next step would either make him fall or make him fly like a bird that soars high like a hero. It smiles, it sings and its heart is always filled with joy. It is free.

By dawn, it was beginning to get bright outside. There were still a few stars in the sky and only a few lights were on in the houses; the earth and the sky seemed to reflect one another in their darkness and light. The darkness of Aysher's life was also like that; in spite of a few positive things, the darkness prevailed. His past haunted him as he started questioning himself, 'Why am I thinking this way? Is this a nervous breakdown? I have often read stories of famous people who suddenly go into hibernation and never come back. Ultimately, we read of their lonely and sad demise from this world.'

When there is a high, then surely there is going to be a low. That's the rule of nature. 'Why am I in this situation? Who wants me to give up? Give up! I have never fallen prey to circumstances. I have been a fighter even as an orphan. People have always praised me, were the praises fake?'

He was in a bad phase with no guide, he closed his eyes again. As he opened his eyes, he had an imaginary conversation with the sun.

'Yes, my child,' said the sun, 'You wanted my guidance? Here I am, like I have been since millions of years. I am the one who informs humans of the day and night. I am a part of everything. Look at the small colourful butterfly, it's enjoying the morning with its fellow mates. The river that sounds dangerous at night, leaves its harshness and becomes playful in the morning. Flowers bloom, birds chirp, the breeze blows and the plants and trees dance with it. Such a beauty. Nature is the most inspiring creation of God.'

A virtual conversation continued, 'But what do I do? How will nature save me from my situation? The humans around me would drag me again into the same old world.'

And then with open arms the sun said, 'Come to me, son, and I will answer all your questions.'

Aysher planned to leave himself in the arms of nature and follow its tune, to rejuvenate as a powerful child of God.

Aysher got ready for his expedition which had no path nor destination. As he looked all around the room full of all materialistic objects, he felt no inclination towards any of them. He got dressed and sat on the study table to write a letter to Risha.

Dear Risha,

I know you have constantly made an effort to sort things out between us, but that will not be possible till I sort myself out as a person. I am mentally shattered, and frankly I am not in the condition to take a decision. My wrongdoings have drained me and that has taken a toll on my mental peace.

I think you also need some time to think practically before taking any sensitive decision. I have taken my decision and you are free to take yours. I will always love you, and all the best for whatever you do.

I am going to an unknown destination for some time. Please do not try to look for me. I will be fine with your good wishes.

I hope you will understand. Wish you all the luck. Take care.

Aysher.

He kept the letter on the bed along with his mobile phone and wallet. He packed some basic items and a water bottle. On second thoughts, he took out some cash from his wallet and kept it in his bag. He wondered if his identity was just limited to the small identity cards in his wallet. Was he nothing beyond that? He felt as if he was freeing himself from all the materialistic chains he had tied himself in. He opened the door and went out not knowing when to return.

There was still some time left for the sun to come out and engulf the darkness, and bring life to each particle. Aysher could not decide which direction to take. The surroundings were all calm and peaceful. He sat on a milestone by the side of the road. Slowly the sun rose like a king.

It was almost as if Aysher was hypnotised; he rose and walked in the direction of the sun. He crossed populous areas, and saw a lot of things that made him thoughtful.

He stopped to notice all the nature around him; the trees were a symbol of tenderness, purity, simplicity. They never use hatred or cunningness amongst each other and they live and let live. They even welcome the animals that come seeking shelter.

He stopped for a bit, drank some water and walked on.

He remembered his first day at work. He remembered entering his boss' room as an intern—his boss in his late forties looked towards him, with soul piercing eyes and it seemed that he could read each of Aysher's thoughts.

Aysher topped his media college and was recruited by the best media house. He remembered tearing up when his boss started asking him questions; he tried to control them but couldn't stop. After some time, he was sent to his work station and from there, there was no looking back.

His work was beginning to be appreciated by his co-workers. One day, his boss called him in for some coffee and talked to him about a lot of things relating to office, people, work, and his family background. Later when Aysher was about to leave, his boss said, 'and I hope now you have built up the confidence to answer questions without moistening your eyes.' To Aysher's amazement, his boss had noticed his anxiety and still gave him the time and space to adjust and learn. College is where you learn a lot; you discuss, debate, compete, answer questions but still you are in a protected environment and the people around you are at the same intellectual level. In office, one is on his own, like an orphan who has no one to fall back on.

His boss was a gentle soul. He nurtured and groomed Aysher and always encouraged him to do better.

'Arise, go forth, and conquer,' something his boss had written to him on a piece of paper, became his mantra and that's what he kept doing for all these years.

Chapter 5

*W*HEN HIS thoughts left his mind, he realized that he was walking on the main road.

Walking for the next few kilometres brought him to a small shed. His footsteps became faster as he felt hungry. As he was approaching the shed, it appeared to him like a house outside which a small table and chairs were laid out. He waited on the chair for some time and when no one approached him, he walked towards a counter of sorts. He could clearly hear noises coming from the inside of the house. He pushed the window open and as he peeped inside, he saw an old lady in her late seventies sleeping peacefully. He didn't want to wake her up but she was the only one who could help him. He knocked at the window and she woke up in amazement.

Her white hair was tied in a small bun, she was fair and her face was wrinkled. She still seemed very sleepy but had a welcoming smile. She looked at Aysher from head to toe and then signalled him to sit outside.

Aysher went and sat outside on the chair, the wind had now become warm but it still seemed pleasant. The old lady approached him after a few minutes and asked, 'What do you want, stranger?' Aysher said, 'I am very thirsty and would like some water to drink.' 'You wait, I will get some fresh water for you,' said the old lady and went in. She came out with a jug of water. Aysher soon drank more than half of the jug and poured the rest into his bottle. When he was about to thank the old lady, she extended her hand towards him. Aysher could not understand her gesture and looked at her questioningly. 'Ten rupees,' she said. Aysher replied in amazement, 'I haven't eaten anything here.' To which the old lady replied, 'This is for the water. In the hills, water does not come from the tap. My family and I have to make a lot of effort to go and fetch it from the stream. This is not free.' She was right. Aysher took out a five hundred rupee note and gave it to the lady. 'I respect your effort, thank you for the water. I am very hungry. Can you please give me some food? I have a long journey.' The old lady smiled and answered, 'Sure, I will make something for you but that will take some time. Please sit,' and again went inside holding the prized five hundred rupee note in her hand.

The breeze was making its presence felt. Aysher's mind was blank. Back in the city, he was always racing with time; this feeling of having nothing to do made him uneasy and a little giddy. It had been years since he had been this idle. Aysher looked around, examined his hands, got bored, took out his wallet and kept it back.

He wanted to take a nap but his hunger kept him up. Aysher looked around the surroundings—the ground was covered with wild grass and flowers, there was not even a small patch of barren land. The place had lush green, tall trees. A tree caught Aysher's attention because of its beautiful purple flowers. Just then, his eyes fell on a squirrel which ran from one direction to the other.

Its innocence, quickness and agility caught his eye. It climbed up the tree, and then quickly came running down and went to some other direction. While running it suddenly stopped, got hold of some food, ate it and then again started running around. The little animal did all strange activities but was not being judged by anyone. It was free in every sense. And humans are never free, they are always slaves to their surroundings.

We are tied up by chains of manners, attire, behaviour, language and become prisoners. Then how are we improving, and in what sense? We are making high-rise buildings, high-tech machines. Is this freedom? The truth is that we are not even free while sleeping, as all these gadgets still connect us to the world. We are slaves to our machines, situations and mind.

By this time, the old lady came with his lunch. The smell of the food reached Aysher before the lady kept it in front of him. She placed the plate on the table with a smile. It was a steel plate heaped with hot chapattis and a big bowl of vegetables. The food looked simple but had an irresistible fragrance and in no time, Aysher started to stuff his mouth. He let off a smile of satisfaction.

When the lady came out with a jug of water, Aysher said, 'The food is really tasty, I have never had this kind of food.' She filled his glass with water and replied, 'That is because of the atmosphere; the fresh air and the energy of the hills affect the food's taste.' 'I was really hungry, I thank you for the food again,' said Aysher. In the meanwhile, the old lady packed some more food and handed it over to him and said, 'Keep it, you might need it.' Aysher again thanked her and enquired about the distance to the next town. He quickened his steps towards his next destination.

The path towards the town was untouched and pristine. It was a narrow path between a dense cover of trees and bushes; it was almost like walking into a green cave. The trees had a scent that was enchanting. In his many journeys, Aysher had seen both gigantic peaks and the deepest points on land. The height and the depth are, in a sense, married to each other. Life is also like that—the ups and the downs are both its phases. The hills teach us to be strong and determined, yet to remain calm and peaceful.

But this journey was different; he was walking towards nowhere. His hair was flying in the breeze, his heart and mind felt light never like before, and he sang some unknown tune. The only thought that crossed his mind was that life was good, even when he was on his own.

As the sunlight started to fade, he began worrying about his legs. There were still a few kilometres left to reach the town. The thick canopy of trees started to get thinner and it meant the presence of humans who had cut trees for their requirements.

It was about 6:30 in the evening when Aysher reached the town. Lights and the oil lamps twinkled here and there; the population of the town did not seem to be much. One or two vehicles drove past him, and the sound of the radio could be heard coming from the distance. Aysher had started to enjoy the lonely walks through jungles as these were bringing him closer to himself. It was also relieving him from the stress that had continuously harrowed him. Man is really a social animal, he felt safe among strangers.

He was totally exhausted after such a long walk and each and every bone and muscle throbbed with pain.

Evening is the time when all animals want to go back to

their cosy homes, but Aysher was still walking. He walked slowly as he was looking for a place where he could spend the night. While walking, he reached a small shop; he went and sat on one of the chairs. He was soon attended to by a boy; Aysher ordered a cup of tea. The boy shouted to the man in the kitchen, 'Table number two, one cup tea' and went on to wipe another table.

The boy's clothes caught Aysher's attention—his jeans, jacket and scarf were all very trendy. The golden streaks in his hair complemented his complexion. After some time, the same boy got him a cup of tea. The weather had started to become colder and the steaming hot tea felt even more comforting. Aysher had learnt a very important lesson in life; success is only possible in the presence of critics, and survival is only possible in the presence of company. Without company, it is difficult to even exist.

During college, drinking tea used to be his signature statement. They discussed revolutions while sipping tea in the canteen. One of his professors had said, 'Life will teach you more than I ever could.'

Getting a job through campus placement was easy for him, but as he entered the office premises, he had to change many things about himself. He traded his kurtas for formal wear, coffee took over tea and all he could think of, were the demands of viewers and TRPs.

His work required him to slog for hours. He was getting promotions very fast and before most of his co-workers, but chasing deadlines was draining the spark out of his life. He worked like a machine to accomplish the targets with no time to think of his own future. .

And now, he was sitting here, amidst strangers, feeling secure in their presence and leaving his whole life behind. There were only two things that could happen—either the path would help him find himself or he would lose his way completely. Maybe destiny could even bring him close to death. A shiver ran down his body, while he wandered alone in the woods. He couldn't imagine dying alone in these woods.

God bless the boy who interrupted his weird thoughts, 'Is there anything else I can serve you?' he inquired. The best way to get rid of unwanted thoughts is to do something new. So Aysher answered, 'Yes, can I get a place to spend the night?' The boy replied, 'Yes, we have two rooms at the back of our house, but I have to ask my father and then can let you know.' Aysher was extremely tired and wanted some place to rest, so he nodded his head, and the boy went on to make further enquiries for the room.

While the boy talked to the man at the counter, his thoughts again raced back and started to question him. He thought, 'What am I doing here? What is it that I want? What will I get in return? Are the efforts worthy?' Aysher got caught in the cobweb of questions.

But some things were very clear in his mind. He was not happy with the life in the city.

Aysher looked up at the sky; he saw a lot of stars twinkling. Just then the boy came back. Aysher picked up his belongings and followed the young guide to the room.

The room was made of wood, it had no fan and just a small bulb hanging in the middle of the ceiling. There was a small bed with a chequered blanket. It had two cane chairs and a very small balcony. The boy then informed him that if he required anything, he just had to knock on the right wall of the room. The room on the other side of the wall was the kitchen and there was always someone from the family there. He also told him that all the meals were served on the front counter.

The room was a private one and had a small glass window. Aysher placed his shoulder bag on one of the chairs and sat on the other. It was cosy and warm.

Aysher planned to wind up for the day and after freshening up, headed towards the counter for dinner. The man sitting at the counter was busy counting his earnings. He saw Aysher and they both exchanged smiles. He signalled him to sit down, and called out, 'Sanjay, get dinner for the guest.' The breeze had now become chilly. Aysher was enjoying it when the boy, came in with his dinner.

Aysher was amongst strangers but they were simple and friendly people.

Aysher had wandered the whole day to reach this place. It was such a different feeling for him. In the morning, he was among people who knew him very well, and by the evening, he was in an unknown place with absolute strangers.

As he lay on the bed, he could only hear the sound of the breeze accompanied with the sound of some insects. No traffic sounds. His muscles loosened and in no time, he dozed off, not knowing what the next day had in store.

Aysher's sleep was broken by a sharp and straight light that pierced into his shut eyelids. The disturbance irritated him, and he wanted to shout at the person. But as he opened his eyes, it was a sight to behold; the most amazing and breathtaking sight of his lifetime!

The glass window in front of the bed became the canvas

on which the painter had painted. Aysher was stupefied. The view hypnotised him as he sat upright on the bed with eyes wide open, observing the creation of the creator.

There was a full mountain range in front of him, with the sun peeping behind it. There were many rows of mountains. The first row had trees, roads, houses. The clouds were spread like fluffy cotton balls here and there. The second range was barely visible and only its snow-clad peaks could be seen. The third range was somewhat visible only if one looked hard. The sight was just mesmerizing.

It took him a long time to realize that he was feeling cold. Aysher covered his body with the blanket, rested his back by the wooden wall and again viewed the beauty of nature.

After some time he realized that a small patch of sunlight was on his bed. Aysher shifted towards the soothing sun rays and curled himself like a baby to fit into his mother's lap, and drifted into a peaceful slumber.

After some time, the boy came with a breakfast of scrambled egg, parathas, tea and the morning newspaper. Aysher was surprised on receiving the breakfast in his room and looked towards the boy in amazement. Before he could question, the boy answered, 'That's because I am free, so some selfless service,' with a chuckle. 'Thank you, but you can take away the newspaper,' replied Aysher. The boy was amazed and questioningly asked, 'You don't look like someone who does not know how to read!' Aysher replied 'It's not that. I am thinking of something else at this point. Can you tell me some of the beautiful places I could visit nearby?' To this the boy answered, 'There is a lovers' point, a small shopping area, a small restaurant.' 'No! Not these kind of places,' interrupted Aysher.

Then, Aysher used his reporter's skill and asked, 'Ok, so you must have been to all the places you mentioned just now,' said Aysher. 'What a stupid question! I belong to this place and I have been to all these places,' answered the boy with a laugh. Now came the question which Aysher wanted to ask. He slowly framed it and said, 'There must be some place of which you just know stories and you still haven't been there.' This made the boy think and after some thinking, he said, 'Yes, there is a place about which my grandfather used to tell me. He had been there in his teenage days along with his friends. He promised to take me there but could not,' and sadness gripped his face. Sensing the emotional situation, Aysher kept his plate down and got up to hug the young chap. After a few seconds the boy continued, 'It's called the Valley of Flowers, my grandfather used to tell me that the terrain is quite rough and only good souls can reach that place. It is guarded by angels. If you are lucky, you will be able to see thousands and thousands of varieties of wild flowers growing in the same valley,' said the boy. Aysher again questioned him, 'Do you know the way to this valley?' He again smiled and said, 'If I knew, I would have gone to that place. My grandfather used to tell me the direction by indicating towards the mountain ranges.' After that the boy picked up the newspaper and went away.

'Valley of Flowers...Valley of Flowers...' that is all he could think of. Aysher's appetite vanished. That place would definitely create an everlasting effect on his lost self. It could revive his energies and, maybe, help him return to his normal life.

Aysher's mind was not still. He was constantly thinking. In the end, he said to himself, 'So be it! Tomorrow morning I will proceed to a known destination but, with an unknown path.'

Aysher thought about his friends, especially Risha; it would have been so difficult for her to continue with her routine. It was he who had lost all interest in life, why should she pay the price for his faults? Risha was always there for him but he had usually abandoned her. She was the closest to him and yet, Aysher had kept her so far away from him. Then, the feeling of being a coward gripped him and he started to feel extremely guilty. He promised himself that whenever he got done with his quest for peace, he would first go and meet Risha.

Destiny takes one to unknown destinations, there are a few things that we decide in life and few that are already decided by God. Once a flower grows, it has to wither away; no matter how beautiful it was, it can never regain the beauty nature had taken away from it. And if it was destined to relive, nature would again give it life.

Chapter 6

𝒯HE NEXT morning was different for Aysher; he was feeling relaxed and determined to see this exotic place. The excitement made him happier. 'Valley of flowers,' the name itself was so mesmerizing. He went out to the small balcony—just to have a look at the weather. It was a beautiful day, with no fog but there was a strong breeze. The sky was fully covered with clouds and birds were chirping in the backdrop. He hurried back to get ready for the long day.

From what he gathered from asking around, Aysher figured that the locals only had a faint idea of where the valley of flowers was.

He was happy to find a short term goal and hoped to revive his energies and get back to the journey called life; a journey where he had a companion Risha, who he had left alone. Even a small hope could go a long way in transforming life. Today, Aysher had the same feeling of getting ready for work back in the city, ready to accept a day full of challenges.

As he stepped out of the room the sharp sun rays almost blinded his vision. In cities, the sun only becomes a source of light; Aysher had not looked straight at the sun for years. He felt the sun rays on his body; awakening each part, illuminating each corner and filling all of it up with light. He closed his eyes, stretched out his arms. The dull, lethargic, old and discharged machine-like body of Aysher had been touched by a source of energy.

He stood there as if in a trance for some time, he found it difficult to walk, and he sat on the ground leaning against the wall.

It was about noon that Aysher realized that he was late and hurried in the direction of his destination. The rocks had started to heat up and it was becoming difficult to walk. The sun was shining bright with no sight of clouds. Aysher thought of taking a short cut as he could clearly see the next road and also because the short cut seemed shaded, peaceful and beautiful.

In no time, Aysher reached the next road. Now this seemed fun to him. He continued to take short cuts. He stopped at one shop and enjoyed his lunch and made a few enquiries about his journey. Some people at the shop advised him to stop at that point and proceed in the morning, but Aysher wanted to visit the valley that day itself, and come back and stay at this point for the night.

The way ahead was an uphill climb and required a lot of energy. His legs had started to pain and his feet had swollen, so he loosened his laces. Some thorny bushes had scratched his hands. He was a workaholic, he had achieved a lot of targets but had never done something like this before.

After walking for some distance, even taking one step further was becoming difficult, but the thought of the jungle and wild animals scared him. By that time the heat of the sun had decreased and there was a cool breeze blowing, bringing him some relief. He was fully exhausted, but walking was the only way out of the situation, and so he continued to walk.

Excess of everything is bad and Aysher understood it when he was trapped by it. When you overload yourself with work, first your body gets tired and then it takes over your mind. The gentle breeze was giving him a lot of relief while walking; the weather was changing from a hot day to a cold evening. The breeze had picked up some moisture, Aysher could make out that it might be raining somewhere close by.

He longed to see a human being; his water and packet of dry fruits had finished.

Things were falling apart, and sunset was just an hour away. He was continuously walking so that he could be out of the place but this shortcut seemed to be never ending. His body ached but he kept the pace of his legs, just then something struck him—why doesn't this short cut end? What road was this?

'Am I on the wrong track?' 'Have I lost my way?' This feeling came over him like a glacier. He realized that it had been quite long that he had entered this so called 'short cut'. In just a fraction of a second, he was sure that he was in the middle of a jungle and had lost his way. It was a frightening situation for him. The pain in his legs vanished as there were other things that the mind prioritised.

He quickened his pace and after walking for another kilometre, he realized that the steepness of the slope had reduced. The height of the trees had also reduced and there were thorny bushes all around.

Slowly the bushy area also came to an end, and soon he stood on a flat. A flat hilltop was the last thing he had imagined to run into here. After a couple of steps, he could feel that the end of the plateau was near. The sight that lay in front of him filled his heart with dismay. The hill on his side had a steep slope; it was like being stuck between the devil and the deep sea. On one side lay the dense forest that was impossible to cross, and on the other side, was the vertical slope.

He was standing on top of a hill, with no food and water, the sun was setting in front of his eyes. The only option was to get down the slope. 'Only if I get down the slope safely, will I reach the valley. I am not a mountaineer, how will I do that?' he asked himself. With the faint sunlight that was left, all he could make out was that the valley had a river and one or two huts by its side. His goal, was to reach one of the huts as soon as he could.

Just to check the steepness of the slope, he rolled down a rock. It rolled down fast and vanished after a few seconds. He knew that even a small mistake could land him into the arms of death. Without any prior experience, he stepped forward but didn't know which direction to take. Aysher had never done rock climbing, but all he could recollect were actors doing it in movies. They usually face the hill and hold on to some stems and roots. He did the same and started getting down the slope—he held on to some roots, keeping his feet on the firm rocks he went a bit lower, closer to his destination. He was keeping up his pace and soon the plateau could not be seen. Mind is the best company one can have in a crisis situation, but one should not lose faith and hope.

Aysher continued his descent. He was doing great but just then a small droplet landed on his hand. Nothing worse could have happened; Aysher looked up only to find that the whole area was covered with dark grey clouds.

The whole descent was about four to five kilometres and

he had already crossed about three. The sun was setting right in front of his eyes. When only a few minutes were left, he stopped and looked around the whole place. Nature at sunrise looks so pure, serene and vibrant, but at sunset it looked horrifying. The visibility had decreased by then, just the twilight was left. Aysher knew that in no time the place would become as dark as a dungeon.

Blood started to rush down his veins, his heart beat increased and he started breathing heavily. It had begun to drizzle. Some things appear good in favourable situations; if the drizzle started when he was indoors, he would have enjoyed it with a hot cup of tea. But now it seemed like a curse.

In no time, the place became pitch dark. Aysher wondered why God hadn't given us eyes like bats so that we could see in the dark. Slowly his visibility went to zero, he could not see a thing and could just feel now. To hold on to a root or stem, he first had to check its strength by pulling it, then find a proper place that could hold his feet. Due to this, his descent took longer.

To boost up his energy and confidence he started to make sounds like 'Yeh!', 'Good!', 'Come on!', 'Yo!' He was behaving like a human chimpanzee. The first few steps were of course not easy, but later on he again picked up the pace. A heroic feeling brought him a lot of self-appraisal.

The worst was yet to come. Suddenly, something bit him on his right hand and in reflex action he left the creeper support, not realizing that this could cost him his life. The rock on which he stepped on in haste was also not firm and he was just holding on to one root with both hands, trying hastily to find a support. He tried to move around and find some support of some other creeper but could not find one. The whole body weight and also of his back pack was being borne by that lone fragile root.

Finding no strong support, the root he was holding also loosened, only to break. In a slow motion, Aysher could feel that these were the last few seconds of his life. He was destined to die in this part of the world, and that too alone. His friends would never know what happened to him. He wished he could have gotten one more chance to live his life.

He was falling from a height and remembered the people who cared for him, and longed to meet them.

Chapter 7

*A*YSHER COULD feel something moving on his body. It took him a while to realize that he could still breathe and that a hand was applying something on different parts of his body with care. He could not move his body and had completely lost the feel of his legs. His breathing was very faint and he could not open his eyelids. He had a severe headache. The temperature of the body was quite high and he had very little energy to find out where he was or who was attending to his bruises.

His body was recovering; in a few days, he regained consciousness and tried to move. It was at that point that someone supported him, raised his head a little and asked him to gulp down a warm liquid.

'Have I reached home and is this Risha taking care of me?' he thought. But soon he realized that the attendant was male as he said with concern, 'Relax, son. You are safe. Just try and rest, you will be fine in some time.' He could hear the voice very faintly due to the bandage around his head. He was lying injured in an unknown place, with unknown people around.

Days passed and Aysher could just stay conscious for some minutes. He started to feel grateful for the person who was there for him throughout the day. Each day he could feel that the bandages were changed. He was on a liquid diet, which was very easy for him to gulp down. The first gesture that Aysher could show to the attendant was holding the attendant's hand with a lot of warmth. One day when his sleep got broken, he could hear the ringing of some bells and could feel the sprinkle of water all over his body. He could even smell the incense. He had become used to not opening his eyes, but today his caring attendant said, 'You can open your left eye, son. Today the bandage of that eye has been removed. It is fine now.' Aysher opened his eyes after days; he could see the daylight, after so many days of darkness.

On opening his eyes he saw a man in his fifties—fair, grey hair with an extremely caring smile. He helped Aysher raise his head and asked him to take that same warm liquid once again. After resting his head on a high pillow, Aysher said, 'Thank you, for saving my life,' tears of gratitude twinkled in his eyes.

'Speak less, son! The body is still very frail and requires proper rest and medication,' said the attendant. 'I will answer all your questions. My name is Vaidji, and you are in a village named Phulma, you have been here for almost a month. We found you near the village river. When you were brought here, we thought you had an accident. There was very faint sign of life in your body. The first five days were very critical but then you recovered. All thanks to God,' he finished his sentence and looked up joining his hands and thanking God.

'Just let me know your name,' he said. 'I am Aysher,' he replied in a very weak and faint voice. 'Your name is very nice, son. You have had a very bad head injury. It requires you to sleep as much as you can. So please sleep. We will talk again.' There was a lot of sincerity in his voice which convinced Aysher, and he obeyed the instructions like a good patient.

When he woke up, he could hear the thundering of the clouds. He was all alone and could see his surroundings with one eye. The room in which he was lying was made of mud; it had two windows and one door. Aysher realized that it was not a room but a whole hut in which he was staying. The hut had no assets in it. It just had an earthen vessel to store water and bedding on which Aysher slept. It seemed quite strange to him but how much does a sick person require, he thought.

The gentle, moist breeze filled the whole atmosphere with positivity. The laughter of the kids, who were probably playing outside, could also be heard. Aysher made an effort to get up and at least sit up, but he was unable to do so.

What felt strange to Aysher that he was not sleeping on a bed; he was sleeping on an elevated platform, also made of mud.

Just then it started to rain and Aysher could see the trees sway in the fresh air and rain falling on them. The weather was such that even a fool could become a poet. Petrichor, a soothing smell of the first raindrops falling on the dry mud, left no scope for him to think about anything depressing. By this time he had lost all feeling of his pains, he was smiling, his heart felt light and it was in tune with the whole atmosphere.

Some moments in life are such that a person wants to hold on to them, but as time stops for no one, the best thing to do at that point is to live that moment to the fullest. One is only left with memories.

While Aysher was enjoying the rains, Vaidji entered. Some people's company is always welcome. Aysher tried to sit up on the mattress taking the support of the wall, the old man helped.

'How are you my son?' he questioned, then smilingly said,

'While you were asleep, Guruji, a very learned man, came and blessed you. He is the guru of the whole village. Today he was passing by and just came to check on us, which he usually does. I wanted you to meet him but he instructed not to wake you up.'

He then smilingly gave Aysher an earthen cup with hot turmeric milk and said, 'An old painkiller, hope you will like it and even if you don't, just gulp it down.' Aysher sipped the milk just to check the flavour, he liked it so much that he finished it in one go, 'It was delicious. Thank you,' said Aysher. Just then the lightning struck and both Vaidji and Aysher looked outside. The weather sometimes is so mesmerizing that no one feels like talking.

'You people are so lucky to live in such a pure atmosphere, the people who live in the city can never imagine a lifestyle of this kind,'said Aysher breaking the silence. 'All this is given to us by our mother nature. She has even blessed you, that's why you are alive. Now your life belongs to her. She will take care of you.' After saying this Vaidji stretched his right hand to bless Aysher by gently stroking his hair. Then he joined hands and looked towards the sky and said, 'O mother of all creatures, bless this child of yours, have mercy.' As soon as the old man said these words, there was again a thundering sound. 'She has blessed you, now you take rest, I will come again.' He helped Aysher lie down on the bed and went out of the hut. Aysher simply had no words for this act.

Short and frequent naps were the best medicine for a recovering person. At dinner time, Vaidji came again, and what he saw brought a broad smile on his face. Aysher was sitting upright on the bed looking much better. 'Hope you had no problem in getting up,' he said. To which Aysher replied, 'I feel good that now at least I could get up on my own. But what caught my attention was this white line circled around my bed.' The old man laughed and replied, 'Oh! This line, I came back to just check and you were fast asleep. I saw a caterpillar near your bed spread and drew this line around your bed.' He started to lay down dinner for Aysher and continued to speak, 'The caterpillar is very common in this area during rains. Sometimes it is too irritating.'

Slowly Aysher's focus changed from the conversation to the food that was being laid in front of him; it had been days since he had eaten solid food. The meal was hot, smelt fresh and delicious. The aroma of the food was totally captivating. The dinner contained some chapatis and a vegetable. The food was served on a big banana leaf. After laying down the food the old man said, 'You have not been given food for a long time and so I have just got a small quantity. Sorry for not serving you properly, but we do not have plates in our village.We use banana leaves, please bear with us.'

Aysher replied, 'No, no please do not say so. I truly love the village lifestyle and this experience. It is refreshing, as if I am on a holiday. And can I now start with my meal as I cannot wait for long.' 'Sure,' said the old man affirmatively. As soon as Aysher took a piece of the bread, the old man stopped him by holding his hand and said, 'I am really sorry for this, but son, we have a belief in the village that no food will benefit the body unless it is first offered to God.' Aysher was stunned by this statement and had nothing more to say but, 'I will surely not break the custom, please teach me how.'

The old man instructed him to take a piece of bread and vegetable, keep it by the side of the plate and circle it with a few drops of water. Aysher was then asked to continue his meal. After finishing more than half the meal, he asked Vaidji, 'I have a question for you, is each and every member of the village keeping a piece aside as an offering to the Almighty?' To this, the old man said yes. Then again Aysher questioned, 'Then in that case, the whole village is throwing away a meal for twenty people?' To which Vaidji said, 'No, we do not waste even a bit, please continue your meal and you will surely get the answer in a few minutes.'

Aysher was just about to finish his meal when two girls in their teens came inside. They both had a small basket in their hands. They smilingly came, picked up the offering, kept it in the basket and went out. The old man said, 'I hope you have a faint idea that we have a place where we regularly keep all the food given as offering to God. Numerous animals come and eat that. These animals also need food like us and if we give them food, they do not come into the village and disturb us. Someday I will take you to that place, it is a very engrossing sight.'

Aysher listened to Vaidji in complete attention. It had only been a day since he had gained consciousness, and the more he knew about these village people, the more he got amazed by such simple and yet so amazing lifestyle.

Vaidji came back after some time with Aysher's medicine and was accompanied by a little girl. The old man sat beside him and started dressing his wounds. 'Your wounds have partially healed but that is just the outer layer, the inner bones and muscles need more time and medication. Give me the leaves in the basket Jaya, she is my granddaughter, she wanted to see you.' The girl looked at Aysher and smiled, he too smiled back.

It was for the first time that Aysher was seeing his wounds;

they were a combination of infected bruises and open wounds caused by sharp objects. There were also some small but painful wounds that were also caused due to penetration of thorns, some deep cut wounds, and some small bite wounds. Vaidji wiped them, cleaning all the previous medicine and they became clearer. The small bites here and there attracted Aysher's attention and he tried to touch one of those. 'Oh no, don't do that. That might increase the infection, danger might have gone but remember you are still on the way to recovery.' Aysher slowly withdrew his hand, questioned the old man, 'What kind of bites are these?' To which Vaidji answered, 'These are all sorts of insect bites—scorpions, ants, may be some semi-poisonous snakes, some leeches. When you were brought to the village, your whole body was pale. We were really worried about you. For five to six days you did not show any positive sign. But later you started to recover. It was the wish of the Almighty that you recovered.'

After some time he turned towards Jaya and instructed her to get a bag from his hut. Jaya went out and came back with Aysher's bag, his sole companion on the journey. He then gave Aysher the bag and said, 'You should thank your bag, son. It was because of the bag that we could find you. Actually you fell into the bushes and your bag fell into the stream, our water source. It was from your bag that we came to know of your presence and on searching for you extensively, we found you in deep bushes, all wounded.' Aysher thanked Vaidji for the bag and kept it aside. 'I wanted to ask you one more thing, son. Is there any family member that you want us to inform about your accident? We can make a phone call on your behalf from the PCO of a distant town. Actually, some of the villagers keep going to the nearby town to sell handicrafts made by us and bring along some items. They can make a call,' said Vaidji in a concerned voice. 'I am thankful for your concern but by the will of God, I have no close family member to be informed. There are some who worry about me and so I do not want to make them more worried,' replied Aysher taking a deep breath. Seeing Aysher in a thoughtful mood Vaidji did not question and got up to leave when Aysher asked him, 'When will I be able to walk? I want to see the village and meet the people,' to which the old man answered, 'sure that can be arranged, you can be taken outside the hut where you can see the surroundings and the people. Now rest,' and he left along with Jaya.

Chapter 8

*W*E USUALLY do not realize the benefits of our body, and only look after this amazing machine when it needs servicing, after being dysfunctional. The next morning, it felt much easier to sit upright on the bed but standing on the feet without the support of anything was the real challenge.

As Vaidji entered, Aysher delightfully said, 'I was waiting for you very eagerly today. I am going to see the village that saved my life and also meet the people.' To this Vaidji laughingly asked, 'What do you think you are going to see outside?' Aysher thought for a few seconds and said, 'Just a simple village.' 'Ok, then let us see if we meet your expectations or not,' said Vaidji in a zestful manner.

His legs had not been used for very long. Modern science would diagnose Aysher with multiple wounds and fractures. But with the completely natural treatment he received, Aysher's body had only bandages of different kinds.

With a lot of effort and pain, Aysher reached the door of the hut. The weather outside was totally different from the inside of the hut. The free flow of air and the throbbing energy was amazing.

Vaidji made him sit on a little bench like platform and slowly helped him stretch his legs on the platform. 'Always keep your legs in a horizontal position till I say you can fold them, this will help your damaged muscles to repair fast.'

The scene in front of his eyes had left him with no words. He was amazed. 'This is heaven,' he said and looked towards Vaidji, who was sitting by his side.

He remembered the efforts, the pains and the struggle he had to put in to make this village his own masterpiece. Aysher looked towards Vaidji, and judging the situation, decided to keep quiet.

The village had a huge platform in the middle, it was surrounded by a walking path and then there was line of the huts. The huts were all of the same size and shape. At that time, Aysher could see at least eighteen to twenty people on the platform.

'I know you have a lot questions lined up for me. Let me first tell you a story, story of the reincarnation of the village,' said Vaidji.

And he started, 'An abrupt end always leads to a perfect beginning and that was what happened with our village. The story goes back twenty-three years. It was a stormy afternoon, when a woman who was cooking for her family in her hut. She used a mud stove with wood for cooking. The weather was stormy and rugged. She was cooking in a hurry because if the storm grew fiercer, she would not be able to cook for her family. When she was just about to finish cooking, a small spark of fire carried by wind landed on the roof of her hut. Soon the whole village caught fire and the residents could not do much to save each other.'

'That day, every family of the village lost members. Some

lost their mothers or fathers. What was left in front of us, was a paralyzed setup. Incomplete families, there was not a single soul in the village who was not crying. Each and every member had voids in their lives. The village was reduced to ashes, with only half of its population left. We had very little food to eat and faced losses that could never be fixed.'

'What we had in hand, were challenges and sorrows to cope with. There were a few who took their surviving family members and left the village, but there were some who stayed back and instead of repenting, we all decided to make our new village. We made a temporary shed for people. Every member did their best to serve the society. The collective loss had brought us closer to one another, as a strong feeling of empathy had developed. Days passed, we helped each other and our society slowly started to take shape. Today our village works on a total different level,' said Vaidji.

'But what I see are the same huts in front of me, with dry rooftops that caused that dreaded incident,' noted Aysher.

'We have solved the problem once and for all, son,' said Vaidji. 'It might not seem so but it has been done. The day you can walk, I will take you and show how we have solved the problem. But now take a short nap, do not overexert your body. I also have some work. Come, I will help you go inside.'

When Vaidji came back after an hour, he saw Aysher in a lot of pain. He crushed a few leaves with his hands and said, 'This might taste bitter but chew it quickly, then eat this piece of jaggery.'

It was evening when Vaidji was lighting the lamp and Aysher got up. Vaidji said, 'You must be finding it difficult to adjust with us but you do not express it, as we are taking care of you. Am I right?' 'No Vaidji, this time you are wrong. Rather I am thankful to God that I have landed in this heaven. It can get difficult if you don't light the lamp as I am not used to the dark.' and both of them laughed. Aysher was feeling very light inside, as his laughter was very pure, natural and selfless. He had not laughed like this since a long, long, time.

'Well, then you should thank the honey bee for this lamp, son,' said Vaidji wittily. 'Honey bee for the lamp? Now this is weird.' questioned Aysher. To this, Vaidji answered 'Well, the Valley of Flowers is close by, and we get our honey and wax from there. We use it in lamps.'

'Woah, these things are so fascinating! When will I be able to go out on my own from this hut and see all these things?' sighed Aysher. Smiling, Vaidji said, 'soon.'

Chapter 9

*I*T WAS after two months of care that Aysher's condition improved. He had even started to do use the washroom on his own. The hut now was turning into a loving home, a place which gave him immense peace.

The wounds needed no bandaging and only needed ointment application.

Vaidji had now become a friend and a guide to him, he knew that Aysher needed external and internal healing, so he taught Aysher a mantra. Aysher used to recite that mantra while sitting alone in the hut.

Aysher was earlier not interested in reciting the mantra. Reading his mind, Vaidji said to him one day, 'Listen, son. If you are not interested in remembering God, what else would interest you? Try to train your mind to find interest in all that you do. Don't do any work for just gain, do it for the love of God.' Aysher replied, 'Your words seem very nice but I have never done anything like this. I have a totally mechanical mind, but not a spiritual one.'

Vaidji laughed a little and said, 'You don't need to have a spiritual but an empty mind. Remove all the stress from your mind. Remove all the likes, dislikes, happiness, sorrow, and needs; keep it still and patient. Just keep your mind empty and God will Himself make it his home.' 'That's all right, but how?' asked Aysher.

One day Vaidji showed him how to make a garland. 'This is how I do it; I say the mantra once and put the needle through a flower. This came naturally to me, no one taught me this. You can also make a garland of all your sorrows and gift it to God, imagine the relief you will feel. On some days, make a garland to thank Him for all His gifts. This will ease out all your pain,' he said.

Tears appeared in Aysher's eyes. Vaidji left him alone with the flowers and the needle to make the garland. Aysher picked up the needle and kept on looking at it for long. His mind had so many thoughts but nothing was clear. He made no garland that day. The next day, Vaidji came in the morning and kept some more fresh flowers and took away the old ones. That day he visited Aysher a number of times, but they didn't talk. Aysher did his daily work and just sat and gazed at the flowers. He was confused, he didn't know what feeling he wanted to make the garland with. Was it sorrow or joy? He was also thinking if this small effort of just making the garland for the Almighty would bring him peace. Will it release him from the burden of his misdoings? Will he come closer to God? Sometimes he wanted to believe all that Vaidji had said and sometimes, he wanted to laugh at it.

The day was coming to an end and Aysher was still perplexed. He did not know what to do. In the night when Vaidji saw the lamp of Aysher's hut still burning, he paid him a visit.

He saw Aysher, still sitting on his bed while the basket

of flowers lay as he had left it. When Vaidji entered the hut, Aysher's face brightened. There was a special bond that developed between them. It started with a bond of a doctor and a patient, then changed to friends, then to a father and a son and now developed into a bond of a guide and his follower.

Vaidji sat down beside him, Aysher helplessly looked at him and said, 'I am confused, I don't know what to do. My heart wants to believe, but my mind refuses to. I have lots of sorrows and the flowers in the basket will fall short if I start making a garland out of them. And if I make a garland of my happiness, then it will be a very small one. I am lost. I was abandoned at a very early age and since then, I have found no hand that could guide me.'

'I totally understand but I can only listen to you. I cannot guide you. You can only be guided by the Almighty. One thing I can tell you, and I would want you to believe in, is that if you want to find God, listen to His directions. Try and listen to your heart. That is the most probable place where He stays. Keep silent, listen to His instructions. Today, I will not say rest but I will ask you to stay awake and listen. He will definitely speak. Make this the last night of your sorrows. Let it all end. Feel your soul, let the sunrise bring along a new Aysher, one who lives for others and as per the instructions of God. Take care, son. May He guide you,' saying that, Vaidji left.

That night Aysher kept thinking about the garland he had to make for the Almighty. God had just given life in his body, but left all the other sections empty. The career he made was his own choice, but would it have been possible to make this career without the body? When it is night and it's dark all around, only then the negative thoughts overpower the mind.

Everything seems negative. Aysher continued to think, in the middle of the night it seemed difficult for him to remain awake. His mind was feeling tired, his head started to pain and eyes became red. He sat taking the support of the wall of his hut, and fell asleep.

It was the first chirp of the bird that woke him up, he hurriedly got up and seeing his flowers, felt sad. He felt guilty for not being able to make the garland. There was still time for the sunrise, he got up and went to sit outside his hut to see the sunrise. As he stepped out, he found one more basket of fresh flowers. Aysher smiled and thinking of Vaidji, sat down beside it. After waiting for some time, the sky started to get reddish, the nature around started to regain life and filled each particle with energy. The air that blew without disturbing any leaf was quite chilly. Aysher was feeling cold, but it had become his habit to watch the sunrise each day, he was there to witness nature's most exclusive wonder that happens each day, and still never loses its charm. It enters his body, it illuminates the darkest and the deepest areas on this earth.

The colour of the sky again changed, it started to become orange and then changed to yellow. Then a small faint line started to show. After which Aysher stood up, joined his hands and waited for the energy source to illuminate his life. The sun rose. Aysher closed his eyes and prayed to the sun god for guidance. He was still confused as to how he should make the garland. He finished his prayer; his body could feel the heat of the sun rays falling on it. Slowly he opened his eyes.

The sun god was still right in front of his eyes as if asking each child of his to face all the hardships of life with a lot of strength. Aysher thought the sun always tells us to start each day as a new life. This is something that everyone knows but to follow it is tough. We always carry the burden of the past days. Sometimes the burden is so heavy that it makes even that new day full of sorrow.

Then a small thing struck his mind, Vaidji always tells him, that this is like your rebirth, then why am I carrying the burden of my past in this new one? God has given me a new life and the company of wonderful people, why was I thinking about what I have not got, whereas I should think what all I have.

He then looked at the fresh flowers that Vaidji had kept for him and picked up the needle to make the garland. The needle already had a long thread in it but it seemed lifeless, Aysher could feel the similarity between his life and the thread. He then looked at the flowers to observe the colour, some were white and some were red. He picked up a red one and carefully passed it across the needle and then across the thread, he carefully chose the combination of white and red flowers. As the garland was half way through, he observed his thread was slowly gaining life.

The minute he finished weaving in all the flowers, he separated the needle and the thread and tied both the ends to complete his garland; his life was now full of positive thoughts. It was a combination of purity and energy. He took a deep breath of relief and promised himself, that from today he will not live in the past but the present. The garland was an offering full of love to God. He kept the garland back and said to himself, 'Oh, God! I love this life, thank you.'

Vaidji was delighted to see the garland complete, his eyes twinkled and he had a huge smile on his face. It was as if his efforts to give Aysher's life a direction had started to take shape. Vaidji could not bear to see a life being wasted in such a manner. He was nurturing Aysher, like his own child.

Vaidji picked up the basket and went inside the hut. Aysher was sitting on his bed, oiling his legs. As Aysher saw Vaidji, he stood up and waited to see the reaction of his mentor, who lovingly came and hugged him. Aysher hugged him back and both were quiet. Vaidji patted on his back like a senior appreciates a junior on his achievement.

'You are ready, son; ready to learn the ways of this village. Today I will take you around. You will meet the people of the village,' he said. What better prize could Aysher get; this is what he wanted since a long time. 'I have to give medicine to an infant who has fever. I will come in some time and we will go together,' he said and left.

Vaidji came after half an hour. He instructed Aysher, 'Listen, son. I am taking you out of the hut because you need a change, but your mind needs different thoughts. Remember that your body is still weak, you will not overstrain your body. Is that a promise?' 'Yes, that is a promise. I will never disobey whatever you say,' Aysher replied. With that confirmation, Vaidji wrapped a warm cloth around Aysher's body and they both went out.

Walking was not easy for Aysher—he was limping even with the support of Vaidji. The view outside was spellbinding. There was a huge platform on which sat the people of the village, they were all sitting in four rows bordering the whole platform. This was the first encounter between Aysher and the villagers, and he was super excited. The platform was rectangular and big enough to accommodate the whole village. As both reached the edge of the platform, Vaidji looked towards Aysher and said, 'Come, son. This is the most sacred place of our village; we pray and dine together in this place. We share all our thoughts here. We also have a small temple of our mother Goddess in that corner. Come.'

The villagers also noticed both of them and a few got up to greet them, someone said, 'Come Vaidji, come son.' As the two of them helped Aysher climb the platform steps, someone said, 'Hope you are feeling better, Aysher.' Aysher was surprised to get such a warm welcome, and also that everyone knew his name. He was given a place to sit and Vaidji sat by his right side and another villager sat on his left. Aysher heard a voice say, 'When the kids are served, someone please serve the guest.' Soon a boy in his mid-twenties came and placed a banana leaf and an earthen cup in front of him.

Aysher liked the way the villagers were treating him but did not want to be called a guest. Soon the process of laying the banana leaves in front of everyone was complete. After that some men and women picked up serving vessels and spoons to serve the food to everyone. Aysher noticed that even while serving, everyone was smiling and doing their work with dedication.

After all the villagers were served, the priest stood up. Vaidji signalled Aysher to join his hands and close his eyes, the villagers recited a short prayer. Aysher was following the villagers, as it was the first time that he was sitting with them to eat. After the prayer was complete, all the villagers took out a bit of food from their plates, and kept it on the floor for the birds and animals.

The food tasted delicious and the company made it even better. It was an amazing experience to be with so many men, women and children all sharing their meal. This sight is usual at places of worship, but here strangers were sharing a meal, like an extended family. It was an experience of a lifetime.

After the meal, Aysher said, 'The more I know about your people, Vaidji, the more I am amazed. Don't you people fight? Don't you have competitive feelings against each other?'

Vaidji thought for some time and said, 'Actually, this system has been going on for many years, son. I have been a part of this system since my younger days. For me it is difficult to think out of this system now. You will be amazed when you see what I am going to show you today.' Smiling, he said, 'You were asking me that day how we saved the village from not catching fire again? Come, let me show you something.'

Aysher was walking with Vaidji's support but his legs had started to pain a little. He was walking after a long time.

Then they took a turn and crossed a field and vegetable garden, and reached a small stream which they crossed via a bridge. Aysher loved all that he saw and wanted to spend more time looking around. As they got off the bridge, they reached a huge hut made of mud. 'Here lies the basic answer to all your questions, come in and see,' he said.

They went inside the hut, and Aysher saw many men and women cooking food in huge vessels. Some were busy cutting vegetables and some were washing big utensils. Some were running from one direction to another carrying things. Aysher looked at Vaidji and said, 'Do we have a feast in the evening?' Vaidji signalled him to sit down. He felt relieved after sitting down. 'Now let me speak, before you start off with your questions,' said Vaidji.

'This is our common storehouse and kitchen, son. The grains, fruits and vegetables that we grow are all stored here. Our village and this place is divided by the river. In case there is a fire, it will not be able to cross and reach the village.

The food is cooked according to a set menu that changes each month according to the weather. Everything is equally distributed amongst all villagers. Every member is given equal importance and special care is taken to accommodate everyone's likes and dislikes. Food is served according to the appetite of each member. You might think these things can cause frequent quarrels, but I would say that we are simple people and if we get our share of food or know someone else needs it more than us, we villagers happily share our portion rather than fighting over it. Loving each member as our own family member is something all of us are taught as children. For you it might be strange, but for us, your lifestyle is strange. We love our life and do all things as a service to God and His children.'

It took Aysher a few seconds to understand what he heard. He murmured, 'You people have a common storehouse and a common kitchen, a thing so rare in the cities.' He thought about how these people have achieved such impossible things with such simplicity. This is an achievement. He turned towards Vaidji and said, 'You know Vaidji, what you people have achieved, is a solution to a very big problem. In cities no one wants to live in a big family; everyone wants a nuclear family. Even children are not ready to live with parents after a certain age.

'You villagers are not cultivating crops, you are cultivating love and affection for your peers,' continued Aysher. 'Yes that is true,' said Vaidji in an affirmative voice, 'Do you see these people sweating in the heat? This is because they are concerned about the hunger of others, they are dedicated towards their work. They are not stressed because someone else is looking out for them.' 'There is no one in this world who is stress free, I can bet on it,' said Aysher.

'You are talking about the city people, son. They have specific boundaries and everyone is focussed on increasing their property. But here we extend the boundaries of our love,' said Vaidji and smiled.

'There are a lot of duties that have to be handled in our village so we have created specific departments. Little children whose mothers are at work are taken care by old ladies, old men teach the younger ones and provide them the basic education. People can choose from the department of their choice like pottery, farming, tailoring, cooking, taking care of the cows, maintenance work, making bamboo ware, weaving; we also have a department that sells some of our hand made products in the town market, and buy what is required in the village. It is difficult to understand, but the villagers will tell you that all of them are happy. You can say, we live in a very big house in different rooms; we not only share our food but also our sorrows and our blessings. When someone is in trouble, we face it together, 'said Vaidji.

'I agree with all that you say, Vaidji, but even twins do not do things in the same way. What do you do when one of the village residents do not agree to your ways and wants to go to the town and stay there?' he questioned. Vaidji answered in a very serious voice, 'Yes, it has happened but we have also found a solution. The first time it was tough, we allowed the member to go and live in the town as per their wish. We also helped them in setting up. Some continued to stay, but most of them came back as they were not able to adjust there. Now rarely any one wishes to go away and everyone stays here in this family. Do not think that we are old fashioned, it's only that we do not want to live the life where there is too much ownership, we are happy with these sharing and helping ways. It keeps us close to our mother, close to nature, and close to God. Our needs are less, we demand less from the nature and whatever it gives us, and we share it with our peers. We live amidst mother nature just like all living things, damaging as less as possible and staying peacefully like a child sits in the lap of its mother, confident that it is safe and taken care of.' Then looking at Aysher he said, 'Was it a long lecture? I am sorry,' and got up.

As Aysher headed back to his hut, they did not say a word to each other. The people working in the farms sang a song that could be heard with the sound of the stream water and the birds. Vaidji left Aysher in his hut with instructions to rest.

After he left, Aysher rested for some time as his body was in due to the long walk. It was about evening when he got up and went out of the hut just to see the heaven he was living in. The things that Vaidji had told him about the village, were something that he had never thought and even if he did, he knew bringing it to fruition, would have been a real challenge. But, these villagers were doing it all with such ease. The platform on which they all had breakfast in the morning, was now being used by kids to play. The small temple of the Mother Goddess had a few people sitting and praying.

Just then, a member from the kitchen came and placed a cup of warm milk in his hand and went to the others on the platform. These people looked simple, lived a very simple lifestyle but were the most learned men Aysher had ever met in his life. He kept on thinking, his thoughts were still about the people in the kitchen. 'How can a handful of people cook for a whole village?' this was the height of selflessness.

From the time we humans open our eyes to this world, we see positive and negative people. By each passing day, we get used to the negative energies and devise ways of surviving.

These people living in their own small world have surrounded themselves with all natural things. The basic difference between these village people and the ones living in cities, is that these people are living in the space given to them by God and never crossing boundaries to acquire other's share. And the city dwellers don't realize that they are just one of God's creations, not the only one.

Chapter 10

*J*T WAS dusk and the sky was grey with small patches of clouds when Aysher walked outside his hut and his mind went into a flashback.

How he had started his life in the orphanage, how he was left to bear the burden of life at a very young age. How he had started to join the pieces of his puzzled life. His school days were tough. The lesson he learnt there, was that he was alone and every one was a competitor.

How he used to work hard in college so that he could get a campus placement, how he reached the top of the media house.

Aysher never considered problems to be a hurdle, but saw them as challenges and he was used to accepting and winning every time. He was never bothered with the means of winning those challenges, as his focus was always on wining. Each challenge gave him a feeling of accomplishment and a sense of pride. Problems were like a turning point for him, and so many turns had brought his world upside down and now he had even forgotten where he started from and where was the end.

Aysher took a round of the village and came back to his hut. He sat down on the small platform to take some rest. 'Aysher bhaiya,' said a melodious voice, it was Jaya coming out of the hut, 'I have kept the diya inside and Vaidji was asking if you have taken your milk in the evening.' To which Aysher nodded with a smile. Jaya continued, 'He is busy with a patient and will meet you at dinner. Is there anything else I can do for you?', 'Thank you Jaya, please inform Vaidji that I am fine and will meet him at dinner,' said Aysher.

Jaya nodded and went away while Aysher's eyes followed her as she disappeared in the dark and then he looked back inside his hut. A small diya was illuminating the whole hut, just like a ray of hope; these people were his lifeline.

Aysher's life was like a rose plant. It had an aroma, beautiful flowers and thorns; it was sustained on water and fertilizer. In its youth, its presence enhanced the beauty of the surroundings—its flowers were used for prayers, they were used to make garlands. It felt fulfilled and honoured. When its flowers were used by a young lad as a gift to his girlfriend, it smiled. Days passed beautifully and the seasons changed, less flowers bloomed on its stems, then its leaves started to wither away. One scary evening, it was uprooted and thrown in the garbage.

Its soul cried for help, it howled in misery and pain, but no one came for help. Its stems started to decay. The stems which once bore flowers, were now eaten by insects. Heavy rains washed out the whole place. Its last memories were of floating in the rain water and finally into the drains. It felt weak and miserable, it realized that its end was near and so it surrendered to destiny and God's will.

Days passed and one fine morning, a frail stem germinated and sprang back to life. Gradually, its roots and stem regained strength. When it opened its eyes, it found itself near a shallow stream and as far as it could see, there were only green fields.

It was like a rebirth; it looked at the sky and thanked God for its new life. Aysher was also in the similar phase.

Aysher and Vaidji had become best of companions; they could talk endlessly with each other. Where Aysher admired every quality of Vaidji, Vaidji was blessed with a very obedient student. It is always a blessing to have a good teacher, but also a privilege to get a good student. Both are of equal importance and they complete each other.

As they walked after dinner, the wind had turned cold and the sky was clear with the moon and the stars. Aysher broke the silence and said in a low voice, 'How I wish I was born here, Vaidji.' 'Think that you were born here, son. This life is like your rebirth. When you were brought here, your condition was miserable. We prayed for your health and God granted us our wish. You are from a city and an accident brought you to this place, you have not informed any of your family members and you seem like a recluse. There is something behind the picture, and I don't intend to upset you but, son, I have a request. Stay here longer not like a guest or a patient, but as a member. Staying here can heal your wounds.'

Aysher had tears in his eyes. Vaidji continued, 'Your situation should be put in front of the villagers. When the daily discussions take place on the platform before breakfast, you should make a request. I am positive that your wish will be granted. Let God be the decision maker today. You do your deed and leave the rest for Him to decide. I will wait for you at the platform in the morning, don't be late.' As Vaidji got up to leave, Aysher held his hand and said, 'There are no words for you, you are my anchor. After meeting you, I have found a direction to my life. I will not say I am grateful but I will request you to always be my guide and never leave me alone.' Vaidji smiled, patted his back and left.

Aysher went inside his hut and sat on his bed thinking. 'How will I start? How will I convince them to accept me as a family member? What will they ask me? But one thing was sure, whatever it be, I will take the side of truth,' he thought. Aysher had worked in the media for years, impressing people was his forte. But these people are simple and pure souls. Tricks should not be used on them. What will happen the next day was unknown to Aysher but he thought the force that brought him into the loving care of these people must have arranged for something good. He said a short prayer taught by Vaidji and slept in peace.

Chapter 11

*T*HE NEXT day, there was no line of stress on Aysher's forehead. He was relaxed, happy, fresh and at peace.

Aysher proceeded for breakfast before time. He reached the platform. They used the platform with respect and kept it clean.

There was still time for the villagers to assemble, Aysher looked around and his attention was caught by the small temple. He had not seen the statue of God in there, and so unknowingly he started to move towards it. It was a very small temple—half the height of Aysher. He sat in front of the temple in the dim light of the flickering diya, He could see the statue of the Mother Goddess. The statue seemed to be very old, like the sculptures seen in museums. The Goddess was standing, she had a something in one hand, maybe a flower, and was blessing the devotee with the other hand. It was made up of some black stone.

Aysher sat silently for a very long time, the peace that he felt was priceless. It was enriching his soul. In this fast moving world, it is easy to find anything, but peace is something rare. One's mind moves at a very fast speed, it is the fastest moving device that humans have. It never stays in one place—it jumps from future to past, to present from life incidents, to people from office, work to family problems. Aysher was experiencing that same peace and his mind was at the feet of the Mother Goddess.

'She is our caretaker, our goddess of nature,' said a voice. Aysher turned and saw a lady standing with a baby in her arms. She bent down to offer a flower to the goddess and prayed for a few seconds. Then looking at Aysher she said, 'Your condition was very bad when you were brought here by the villagers. It is the blessing of the mother that you are able to thank Her. I hope you never ever face such an accident in your life.' Aysher smiled after being blessed by an unknown lady, she again lowered her head in front of the goddess and ascended down the platform. People of the village were all loving, caring and at peace.

Aysher also lowered his head to thank the Mother Goddess for the new life and company of these blessed people. He thought that new life can only bloom when he can stay back in this blessed land. He got up and turned to the place where the villagers had started to gather for breakfast. The seating arrangement was complete and when the banana leaves were being distributed to all, Vaidji said to Aysher, 'I have already mentioned to some of the senior villagers that you want to say something, so when the process of food distribution is going on, I will stand and take permission so you can make your request. May God be with you.'

After listening to this, Aysher's heart started to thump faster. He went blank. When he was still thinking, Vaidji got up and said, 'This young boy wants to say something' and he gave Aysher his hand to help him get up. He patted on his back and sat down. There was pin-drop silence and except the people who were serving, Aysher was the only one who was standing.

They all had the same expression of curiosity on their faces. They wanted to hear what Aysher wanted to say, this vibe from the villagers gave him the confidence and he started to speak.

'My name is Aysher and I would like to thank you for the new life that you all have given me. That accident that took place was not a co-incidence, ; there is a story behind it. I used to work in a news channel for years and lost interest in my work. I wanted to run away from my surroundings. My friends noticed the change in me and brought me to a hill station so that an outing could rejuvenate me. My mind was restless even with my friends. I ran away without informing them. My journey had no direction and no destination. On my way, I came to know about the Valley of Flowers and wanted to visit that place. I proceeded on foot taking directions from villagers. I lost my way, it was then I met with an accident and reached this village.'

He paused and lowered his head to start again, 'My parents died when I was a toddler, I was brought up in an orphanage. I had always thought that to survive, one needs to fight it out. I know all that is needed to survive in this world, but I am still unaware of what my parents would have taught me, if they would have been alive. I wish to learn all that as a member of this village. Please accept me as a member, otherwise this new life is of no use.'

After finishing, Aysher looked at the faces of the villagers and everyone had a look of empathy on their faces.

'Your life is very precious, my son,' said a gentle voice. A man got up from his place and walked to Aysher; he was taller and fairer than Aysher, his cheeks were pink. He gently rested his hand on Aysher's shoulders and continued, 'Your life is precious to us also, we have given you rebirth with the blessings of God, and our efforts will only be fruitful if your life flourishes in front of us. I sincerely hope that we are able to inspire you in some way.' He paused for a few seconds and looked towards his people, it was as if the old man was giving voice to their words. The old man then addressed his people with one of his hands still on Aysher's shoulder. 'Please raise your hand if you agree with me, people.' In a flash of a second, all hands were up. They all supported Aysher's stay and were ready to accept him as one of the family members.

Aysher was stunned to see so many hands raised in his favour; there was a time in his life when he had nobody to call as a guardian. The column of guardian was always empty in his forms but today, he had so many guardians, it was difficult to even count the number.

The old man said to Vaidji, 'From now on, you be his guide, Vaidji, and teach him the ways of the village. You are a gentle teacher and he is a serious student.' He then nodded in affirmation and went back to his place.

Both Vaidji and Aysher sat down as it was time to resume the breakfast. After praying and taking out one bite for the animals, everyone resumed the breakfast but Aysher's appetite was lost. Even the aroma of the food could not attract him, Vaidji elbowed him to eat and so he took a few bites, but still he had so many thoughts in his mind. He did not even realize when the food got over.

While walking towards his hut after finishing the breakfast, Aysher felt quite content. Attaining the permission to stay in the village, not as a guest or patient, but as a family member was of utmost importance to him. 'I have some medicines to make if you don't mind, you should go and rest. We will discuss how to engage you, there's lots you have to learn,' said Vaidji. Aysher thought for a second and said, 'What if I join you in making the medicines, I hope you don't mind?' Vaidji answered affirmatively, 'Certainly, son. Come.' Both of them strolled towards Vaidji's hut.

Vaidji's hut was just like any other hut of the village. The door, its height were all the same as Aysher's hut. The inside of the hut was also similar barring some wooden racks which had some bottles. Near the wooden racks, was a small raised platform on which some vessels were kept. It was certainly not his kitchen but his workstation for making medicines. He signalled Aysher to sit near that platform and went to pick some bottles. He carefully selected and brought those bottles to where Aysher was sitting. Some of the bottles had liquid in them and some had a grass like substance in it. Vaidji was meticulously taking out the substances in certain quantities, when Aysher broke the silence by saying, 'So this is where you made all the bitter medicines for me. Whose turn is it today? Not mine, I am sure.' 'No, it's not for you. It's for someone else, replied Vaidji and he started to mix the medicine to make it into a prefect paste. 'Do you live alone Vaidji? There is nobody else in the hut,' questioned Aysher. 'No, son. I live with my wife and an unmarried son. My elder son, who is married, has shifted to another hut after marriage.' Aysher smiled and said, 'The village has also not been able to save itself from nuclear families. This is same as the city life.' Vaidji stopped grinding and looking at Aysher answered, 'No, you are again wrong. My son has not left me and gone, it's the rule of the village that after marriage the son and his wife are shifted to a new hut and are made free to take their own decisions and learn from them. We parents are not a burden for them. And as a father, I am happy the way he and his wife have taken decisions in life, they are still learning and I bless them with my whole heart always.' As the medicine was ready Vaidji said, 'I have to go and give it to the patient, will you come along?'

'Why are the ways of the village so unpredictable? Whenever I think that this time I will definitely catch you, I am again bowled off,' said Aysher. 'Now what happened?' asked Vaidji. And Aysher continued, 'How it that you people can always find solutions for all the problems?'

'Let's walk to my patient's hut, Aysher, and I will tell you why,' said Vaidji. They both started to walk and Vaidji said, 'It's not that we do not have problems, but it's just that we learn from it. A young newly married couple just might not think the way a couple who is married for thirty long years thinks. So it is quite obvious that a problem will occur, so why let it happen. Simple.'

While Vaidji went and treated his patient, Aysher waited under a tree. Seeing that Vaidji might take a little time, Aysher took a short nap. 'I told you to rest, but you wanted to walk with me,' said Vaidji walking up to Aysher. 'I don't have much to do, so I will join you and enjoy the breeze. We also have to make a plan of how you will learn the ways of the village,' he continued.

'I know the basic system of the village or its basic functioning. Then how should I get into that system?' said Aysher.

'Well, then listen, the system is that everyone is given to work in all the departments till he can know the basic nitty-gritty of the departments, and then he is allowed to make a choice.

You also should also start with a department.' 'That's perfectly fine,' exclaimed Aysher. 'There is just one basic problem,' said Vaidji on a serious note. 'And that is?' questioned Aysher. To which he replied, 'It's just that you are not very well right now, and nor do you know all the departments very well. How will you choose in which section you will work first and which will come second?'

'Working in all the departments one by one will make you aware of all the sections. In the end you can make a choice. The day you feel you want a change, even after years of working in one department, you can change. Work satisfaction should be there. Happiness is the basis of living and that is everyone's right. No rule should take it away,' said Vaidji.

'Then I have the answer,' said the highly energized Aysher in a loud voice. 'You make the choice, I know whatever you choose will be perfect for me.'

When a person is alone and he is not happy with the surroundings, he feels very unlucky. Any person who comes close even for a short chat seems like an angel. But when a person has made friends with himself, when he is happy from inside, that is the time when being alone seems like a boon. That is the time one can feel the connection with the soul. As in Aysher's case, now he always had company of his mind, thoughts, his deeds and his soul.

He sat on his bed and drank from the earthen vessel kept by its side. He felt so contented from inside, as if all his senses had touched ice after sweating for days in scorching heat. He slowly stretched his whole body on the floor. He closed his eyes and a small tear of contentment and relaxation rolled down his eyes, and he went to sleep.

The evening was spent chatting with the kids. Chandan, a boy amongst the kids had lots of knowledge, so Aysher casually asked him, 'You are the one who knows most?' to which he answered very quickly, 'If I will not know, how will we function? I have to know everything about my village so that I can be an important part of its machinery.'

Aysher was waiting for Vaidji who would tell him about which department he could work in. As he came, Vaidji said, 'I discussed with some of the senior members of the village, and a majority of them were in favour of you working in a department of your choice. This would help you heal quickly, making you busy will also help you to divert your mind from other things. Lastly, the choice of the department was left to me as I am your doctor.'

Vaidji waited for some time and then continued, 'I will come to take you to your department in the morning.'

'Sitting idle has never been my temperament, it always depresses me and this depression has caused me much harm,' said Aysher while looking at the ground. Vaidji took a long breath and said, 'You are right, son. Depression is very harmful and being active always helps the mind and also the body. This will also help you connect with the village people, you are very close to me but you should know the villagers.' He left with a promise that the next day would open up more avenues for him.

Chapter 12

NEXT MORNING Aysher was applying ointment when Vaidji entered.

'Your department is finalized! I can assure you will love it,' he exclaimed with joy. He took a few steps and sat beside Aysher. 'You will work in the pottery department from today, the department makes vessel, toys and lamps of mud. It will require you to sit and there will be less pressure on your legs. Mud is also a natural healer; it will speed up your healing process.' He kept his hand on Aysher's shoulder and said, 'Remember, son. Mud can heal not only the body, but also mind and the soul.' They both smiled at each other.

Vaidji was a doctor in all senses. He knew that Aysher had been through a lot. He wanted him to relax and guided him in every possible way. On the other hand, Aysher also wanted to concentrate on different perspectives of life, which were still unknown by him. He seemed much eased down but inside, the turmoil, those questions were still there.

That day, like all villagers, Aysher also headed towards his department. 'The potters' department is on a small hillock, and requires one to walk a little, but it is a marvellous place to be,' said Vaidji. Aysher nodded his head and kept following his lead.

At the end of the village road, there was a narrow pavement with wild flowers, shrubs and bushes on both the sides; the path was so thin that only one person could walk on it at a time. Aysher followed Vaidji. The platform had a little slope, and after taking a few steps and a turn, Aysher saw his destination. 'Here it is!' said Vaidji. 'It is so quiet here Vaidji, and the surrounding is so lush green, I love this place!' said Aysher with a bright smile. While walking, Aysher saw hundreds of pots drying in the sun, all of various shapes and sizes. The department was also a hut, just of a bigger size.

There were around seven to eight people working in the hut at different places. Vaidji introduced Aysher to Kashi, a man little older than Aysher. He was tall, fair, his body was lean and he had brown hair. He smiled and said, 'I know you Aysher, you are most welcome to this pottery department. I will try my best to teach you whatever I know.' 'Thank you very much for such a warm welcome, but it is the first time that we are meeting, then how do you know me?' questioned Aysher. 'Well, the whole village knows you, through the speech you made on the platform!' he said. And all three started to laugh.

'Come Aysher, let us start!' said Kashi extending his hand in. Then he looked towards Vaidji and said, 'I will bring him to the platform in the evening, you need not worry Vaidji. I will take full care of your patient.'

After the assurance, Vaidji went away and Kashi took charge of Aysher. Kashi gave him a hammer to break the big chunks of mud into small pieces.

When Aysher held the hammer in his hand, he could feel the weight of the hammer. The rod was made of wood but rest was made up of quite heavy iron. With the first thud Aysher came to know that what seems easy is usually not so easy. With the second, and the third, his hands started to feel the jerk that it gave to the whole body. But as he was a hard working person, he concentrated more on his work and less on his body. When the chunk of mud given to him was fully broken, Kashi asked him to take the roller and grind the broken mud. 'This is better than the previous step as it requires lesser power,' said Aysher looking at Kashi.

After finely grinding the mud, Aysher looked towards Kashi and said, 'I think the mud is ready now.' Kashi nodded and responded in affirmation of the mud being ready and said, 'Now you must collect the mud in this bamboo vessel and take it to the next work station.' Aysher was enjoying all the work, it was the first time he was working with mud. 'Here you need to sieve your mud so that a fine powder is attained,' he said.

Kashi was a very gentle instructor and was guiding Aysher step by step.

Aysher started to mix the mud in different ways and sometimes he even played with it, he experimented with the mixing of the mud. This continued for a long time. The mud was not ice cold but a gentle cold which was taking away all the heat of his hands. The mud was slowly, acting as a pain killer. His pain was slowly reducing and the aroma of the mud was intoxicating him. This activity didn't seem as work, rather it seemed like play.

By this time, his hands were fully covered with mud. The thick mud had formed a coating over his hands. His hands felt smooth, and the enchanting aroma that came from the hands was refreshing. Aysher brought the hands close to his nose and tried to inhale the scent of the mud. His eyes were shut, and after cutting all the connection from the outside world he tried to imbibe the smell. He actually tried to bring the smell deeper inside the body and tried to find a way through which the soul could be touched by the aroma. It was just coming naturally to him, and he was trying to heal his soul which was bruised. Aysher was taking deep breaths; he was actually trying to make a note of the aroma in his mind.

He slowly opened his eyes, and looked at his hands which were now completely dry. The hands seemed very strange, and on a closer look, he got to know that his hands had no lines over them. The mud had covered them all. Aysher thought that, even if I go to an astrologer he will not be able to tell anything about me. Aysher had never gone to an astrologer to know about his future but he always thought that his lines had taken away lots from him. Today all had vanished, his hands had no lines, but one thing was sure that these lines had brought him to the village, and this place was a blessing for him.

After coming out of his thoughts, he looked around and found no one; only Kashi sat in one corner making pots on the wheel. Aysher walked towards Kashi and said, 'I made you wait for long, everyone has gone.' Kashi lifted his head and said, 'I didn't want to disturb you, you were so involved in playing with the mud that I preferred to leave you alone.'

After finishing what he was doing, Kashi got up and started to wash his hands. Aysher was still admiring the beauty of his hands, all his focus was on them. He had never thought about them so seriously. It was today that he realized that his hands were of such a lot of importance. They had always been with him in good times and bad times. Aysher looked up and thanked God for each part of the body. Then he quickly got up and joined Kashi.

While walking towards the village, Kashi questioned, 'Do you want to ask me anything regarding the work you had done all day? If so, you are free, I will be happy to answer.' Aysher smiled and said, 'My questions might seem a little annoying to you.' Kashi directly looked into his eyes and said, 'You don't worry about that, and just think about your questions. My work has brought a lot of patience in me. Let's take up the challenge!' he said in a sporting manner.

'My first and most important question is that how do you people have the same basic and common qualities. I have interacted with many people here and everyone seemed to have some basic qualities. You people never seem like villagers, it seems that I am in company of some learned men. This is the first day that I am interacting with you, still it is so easy to communicate with you.' Aysher just stopped after completing the question, they were very close to the village and he could see the village.

Kashi thought of sitting under the tree just outside the village and answering his question. He thoughtfully said, 'let us sit under this tree for some time, five to ten minutes will not make much difference.' As they sat, Kashi continued, 'Your question is natural, people in the city and village are totally different humans. When a child is born in a city, it sees a lot of competition around, but here in the village, there is no such thing. Rather, we ensure that a child is given the right environment to develop into a beautiful human being and later when he has to choose the kind of job he has to do, he is given a lot of freedom. We villagers do what naturally comes to us and thus are away from all kinds of pressure. Lots of expectations from and desires from others spoil the taste of life for the city people, this is my personal opinion. These desires and expectations when remained unfulfilled, destroy the base of life. The city people smile only when things are in their favour and we smile at everything with nature, friends, family, and kids and with God. The small group of people that you see is not just a village, it is our only world. It is void of all the negativity. I have young kids, but I am not just the only one who is worried about them, rather the whole village is bothered about them. Any kid if found doing any wrong, is taken special care of. His parents are not the one responsible for his deeds rather the whole village is. It is a small, but beautiful world. All this comes to us naturally, as we are very close to our Mother Nature. She is very pure and caring and so are her children.'

'I agree with all that you said Kashi, this is a world in itself and requires no changes. May Mother Nature always shower Her blessings on it, and it keeps on flourishing like this till eternity,' said Aysher. They both smiled and started to walk towards their world where the laughter of the villagers and fragrance of the mouth-watering dinner awaited them.

After dinner, Aysher strolled towards his hut. After reaching his hut he went in and sat on his bed. He gazed outside through the open door. The black dark clouds had already covered the whole sky. It was about to rain any moment. Just then, there was a loud thunder and with it, it started to rain. The drops were big in size and soon, the dry soil was covered with the rain. The soil became wet with each drop and then the scent of the soil started to fill the atmosphere.

This fragrance can never let any feeling stay inside;

everything will naturally come out, no matter how hard you try, because this is the aroma of the meeting of the two extremes, dry and the wet. Anyone who observes this atmosphere is bound to feel two opposites, either very happy or very sad.

The rain brings out different feelings in different people, kids love to dance in the rain and make paper boats. Couples go and enjoy the rain together and the lonely ones sit and just stare at the rain missing their companions immensely. Aysher wanted to stand in the rain and wash off his pains and sins but he just kept staring at the rain.

He stopped his feelings to come out because if they came out, he would not be able to control it. It will be like an outburst, like the outburst of the clouds. He kept on staring outside and without his consent, his eyes started to cry. His cheeks became wet and the trickling of the tears increased. His mind also became blank, he was unable to understand why was he crying. He was continuously wiping his eyes, but tears continued to trickle down. After quite some time, he realized that his back was paining, maybe due to the exertion of the day, so he lied sown on the bed still gazing outside.

The wax lamp was still burning faintly and the sound of the rain had increased. The door of Aysher's hut was open and so some showers also came in with the wind. Aysher was extremely tired, but did not want to sleep. His mind wanted to take him back to the days he had spent in the city, but there are times when you are scared to even think about some things.

Indeed, it was a beautiful place with a great company but still the memories of the earlier life could not be erased from his mind. Aysher thought, 'It was I who ran away from that lifestyle and am I missing it? If yes, why? I was the one on the verge of a breakdown when I ran. I was the one who had created that environment and then, when I had enough of it, I ran away from it.'

These thoughts increased Aysher's heartbeat, he became restless. The feeling of cowardice engulfed him. Why I am so fickle minded, first I ran away from the city life, and now do I again want to run away from the village life. Till when will I run? Will I betray the villagers? They think I am a good person, will I prove them wrong? My friends in the city also thought that I am a good person, but I left them without even informing them. Am I a bad person? Then why do I get all the love just like a good person gets? Even such great company here could not heal my feelings. Aysher wanted to talk to someone but no one was around.

He took a short nap and woke up. Aysher was still feeling the same. The rain had slowed down and it was drizzling, it was still dark outside as there was still time for the sunrise.

Aysher got up from the bed and started to walk in the rain. The drizzling was very faint and he could feel each droplet.

The weather was mesmerizing. Aysher kept on walking for quite some time; he had come out of the village and reached the river side. He sat down on the stone, and dipped his feet in the flowing water. The water was warm and felt very relaxing for his legs. How he wished that the pain in his heart could be dissolved in the same way.

A faint sunlight could be seen in the sky and slowly it covered the whole area, no area was left without light. The night long rain had cleaned everything. Each tree, each leaf was looking fresh. Everything seemed so spic and span. Aysher could see different shades of green; no tree or plant had the same kind of leaf nor did they have the same shade of green. Some leaves had droplets of water on them which shined in the sunlight like pearls. By this time the rain had stopped and small puddles of water could be seen everywhere.

There was a contrast, the weather was happy and Aysher was feeling sad. He could feel his loud heartbeat. 'Heart! Do I have it? Never did I realize its presence,' he said to himself. This was the time Aysher realized that heart is not just an organ but a place where the pure soul rests. There are certain things in life that one does not want to share with others, they are secrets embedded in one's heart.

The stream was flowing, making a musical sound, as if trying to speak to him; it wanted to convey something to him. All the trees, the plants, everything around wanted to say something. Aysher opened his mouth to say something, but the words did not come out. He stammered, closed his eyes and said, 'I am sorry Risha.' Tears trickled down his cheeks but he quickly splashed water from the stream to wash them off.

He again closed his eyes and could see her smiling face in front of his eyes. What attracted Aysher most, were her eyes, her eyes were not big, but very attractive. She had long curled lashes; her eyes were the purest thing Aysher had ever come across. They had nothing fake in them. Her eyes could reflect her feelings, the first day they were introduced to each other, Aysher could make out that she had fallen for him. This gave Aysher a sense of pride. She didn't say anything, but her eyes said it all, the depth of her feelings could be judged just by looking into them. The whole office knew about it, some even warned her. Some said, 'How come Aysher is so lucky to find a person who loves him so truly.' Some were even jealous but nothing deterred Risha from her feelings towards Aysher. In company of others, Risha behaved just like any other colleague but she cared for Aysher more than anyone did in the whole world. She loved Aysher truly; she was kind of a rose that blossomed in a thorny bush.

One day Aysher even overheard a conversation between Risha and one of her close friends. 'Why do you want to waste your time and feelings for the person who cares for none? He is just bothered about his salary and promotions. You are smart, good looking and successful, you can find anyone. Try to look for a person who would love you just like crazy.' To which Risha replied, 'Thanks for your concern dear, but for me Aysher is the only one and always will be. Now nothing can be done.'

After listening to this conversation, Aysher thought for days about it. He felt lucky and also happy that someone was madly and deeply in love with him. He had always been deprived of love and so he thought, maybe God had blessed him this way. These statements of Risha's touched his heart and after a few days, Aysher proposed to Risha while driving home. Risha bought freshness into his life. Slowly, things started to change in his life. He was still sitting by the river side but his mind was churning.

Aysher recalled how during office hours she used to send him small notes like, 'smile', 'relax things will be fine', 'don't be stressed, count backwards'. These things seemed funny, but at that moment it helped him and also drove him crazy for her.

Aysher and Risha were quite different from each other. While Aysher used to play loud music to concentrate on work, Risha preferred instrumental. Aysher was a non-vegetarian but after Risha had come into his life, he also switched to being a vegetarian. She was a girl who had a lot of Indian values. Aysher was not sure, as to how he should ask Risha to stay with him in a live-in relationship. He thought a lot, and so one day, he told her what he had in mind. Initially it was difficult for Risha but she later agreed to it, and that's how they started to stay together.

Aysher was still sitting by the river side engrossed in his thoughts. He was feeling like a culprit, Risha had trusted him such a lot and what had he given her in return? Humiliation. Aysher had betrayed Risha. That feeling was embedded in his heart, a burden on his soul. He kept sitting there for long and later got up and went to join the villagers.

Chapter 13

AYSHER CAME back to his hut from the river side and went to sleep.

When Vaidji could not find Aysher, he got a little worried. He asked a few members if they had seen Aysher but after getting a negative reply, he took both his and Aysher's breakfast and proceeded towards his hut.

The door of the hut was open and Aysher was lying on the bed. Vaidji thought that Aysher had fever and he rushed to his side and placed his hands on his forehead to check the temperature; it was normal.

'Aysher, Aysher, what happened? Why didn't you turn up for the breakfast today?' he asked. Aysher woke up and replied, 'Sorry Vaidji, I did not sleep well during the night. May be because of that, I was unable to get up on time.' 'That's OK, have your breakfast and rush to your work. Otherwise you will be late,' he said.

'You are so caring Vaidji, I am very lucky,' said Aysher emotionally. They had their breakfast but Aysher did not tell Vaidji the reason because of which he could not sleep the previous night.

Aysher soon joined Kashi in the pottery department and

began from where he had left the other day. He was trying to learn to make a simple mud pot on the potter's wheel. The day went by and he kept on trying again and again but could not make the pot of the desired form. Seeing him trying, Kashi also came and supported Aysher saying, 'It is difficult to make a pot on the very second day, these things are tough and might take days, keep trying.'

Aysher was doing something difficult but he adamantly wanted to make the pot that very same day. Actually, he wanted to comfort his mind by doing something in which he was successful. He tried all day and in the evening walked back to his hut. Kashi was observing him all day and came to the conclusion that Aysher would have to join some other department. Pottery was not making him happy, rather he was feeling like a loser.

When the day's work came to an end, Kashi said, 'Why are you taking so much of pressure? If a particular job requires you to work for a few days, then how can you do it in a few hours? You will have to be a superhuman for that. Accept the reality, don't fight with it or think yourself to be a loser. You are expecting too much from yourself. Relax. Come, it's time to go.'

Aysher washed his hands and started to walk towards the village. He didn't even wait for Kashi. There was an emotional turmoil which was disturbing him.

Kashi went straight to Vaidji who was sitting under the tree with a few villagers, and told him all about Aysher's mental frame. This news made Vaidji a bit worried. 'I think you should choose another department for him as he is not enjoying the pottery department,' said Kashi.

One of the villagers said, 'Maybe he is used to working perfectly each day in the office. That's why he had a particular predefined notion that one had to achieve a lot during one day. When he was not able to make pots, a feeling of dissatisfaction made him sad.' One member suggested, 'What if Aysher is taken for a visit to all the departments in the village? Then he can work in the one he chooses.'

With common consent, it was decided that no one would discuss work with Aysher that day.

As he reached the platform for dinner, Vaidji told him, 'Today, we are having a song and dance performance after dinner. You will enjoy it a lot. Finish your dinner quickly,' he said. 'Dance performance? Do you have a singing and dancing department also?' he questioned. 'No, we do these performances every week by rotation. Every family has to perform a song and dance. This is basically done for entertainment. Also, it works as a stress buster, and connects the villagers with one another.' he answered.

Vaidji noticed Aysher was listening to everything but his mind was somewhere else. Aysher was also not enjoying the dinner as much as he usually did.

After the dinner, the place was cleared for the dance performance. The family which came forward had three members. Before starting they joined hands in front of the temple, and then sat down in one end where a mat was spread for them to sit. They started with a song; the song was regarding how much a mother loves her children. The woman was accompanied on a drum by her husband, and her little kid was clapping to give her company. The song was melodious and everyone listened to it, there was pin-drop silence when she sang. It was a simple song with simple words, but it had a very strong effect on all.

After the song was over, it was followed by a dance performance. As there were only three members in the family, some other villagers had opted to join them. They were making sounds with the bamboo sticks, drums and clapping to make music. As the dance started, other villagers joined along. Aysher was also asked to join. It was joy all around as everyone danced with ecstasy, it was wonderful. Aysher was enjoying a lot, but as soon as it ended, he again went back to his gloomy self which was noted by Vaidji.

Vaidji told Aysher to sleep while he sat by his side. Aysher did not oppose this suggestion. He lay down on the bed and shut his eyes. Vaidji got up to inspect the room. He straightened the wick of the burning candle and then checked the ointment that he had made for Aysher to apply on his legs.

The ointment would last for another day and Vaidji thought of making some fresh ointment. He quietly went out of the hut without informing Aysher who was still making an effort to sleep. He went to his hut and collected all the ingredients in a bag, and came back to Aysher's hut. When he came back, Aysher was awake, 'You are still awake? I thought by this time, you will be fast asleep,' he said as he kept his bag in one corner of the hut.

'I am still making an effort, but I am unable to sleep. Can I sit with you for some time?' asked Aysher. Vaidji laughed and replied, 'I know you will not sleep. Come, sit with me while I prepare your medicine.'

Aysher got up from his bed and sat beside Vaidji who started to make his medicine. Aysher thought that these people had accepted him so readily into their village, and were making a lot of effort to teach him the ways of the village. What will happen when they come to know that he was restless here and once again, wanted to run away?

After some time, Vaidji said, 'Rains are quite heavy in this village, as it lies in the valley region. Once it starts raining, it continues for a long time. There is a lot of work left to be completed. Some of the departments suffer due to lack of sunshine.'

'Actually I wanted to speak to you,' said Vaidji. 'There is something that is disturbing you and that is why you are not showing interest in anything. Let me know the reason so that I can help you.'

Aysher heard it all and was still quiet. He did not know where to start from. 'I have a secret...and maybe that is the reason for my discomfort. There was someone else I was sharing my life with...She was my only anchor, my companion and my love. The only love in the world. Her name is Risha.'

Her name could not be heard by Vaidji very clearly as just then, the clouds thundered and the conversation stopped for a few minutes. Vaidji could not hear the name correctly but he could make out that it was about a girl.

'Son, what was her name?' he questioned. 'Risha,' replied Aysher, 'she used to work with me in the news channel.' He said that and stopped. 'Go on, son. Don't let your heart be heavy with the burden of a secret. Let it all come out,' said Vaidji. Receiving support from Vaidji, Aysher again started his story. 'Her name is Risha...'

The story narration went on in the background as the sound of the rain became louder and louder. The heavy heart of Aysher showered all his secrets out in front of Vaidji. After the rain, the clouds became light and swayed away to leave the sky clear.

'I feel that I am the one because of whom the whole problem started, and she must be suffering too,' said Aysher taking a deep breath and ended his story.

After listening to the whole story, it was difficult for Vaidji to comment. He could not understand what to say. 'My dear son, there are times in life when decision making becomes very difficult. And even more difficult is to maintain a normal balanced lifestyle. With my experience, I can tell you about certain important aspects of life,' he paused for a moment and then again continued, 'I will tell you certain things but you have to promise you will listen carefully.'

'Firstly, running away from your situations is one thing I will not approve of. I can understand that you were upset, but running is not the act of an intelligent person. A problem can never be solved this way. When you ran away from the city, only your physical body could run but your mind could not run from there, it is still there. It is still confused and left at a standstill. No matter where you go, your mind will keep you asking the answers to the questions it has.'

'Secondly, you will have to give yourself some time. Follow your normal routine, and keep thinking about what you have in mind. Try a little to divert your mind, and start again. This way you will be able to analyse the situation. Maybe while thinking about it, you will realize your mistakes, and the things you could have done to reduce those. The answers will come automatically. Just be patient and calm. It is difficult to accept, but the truth is that this is just a phase and it will fade away in the long run. Later, you will ask yourself why you were so worried for such issues. Remember, things can either be solved by thinking or communicating.'

It was dawn and the chirping of the birds had started. 'We were talking all night and I wish that the discussion proves to be of use. I will appreciate if you follow your routine today. Will you be able to do that?' asked Vaidji. 'Sure, Vaidji. I will be ready for work and will not let my mental condition come in way of my work,' answered Aysher.

Vaidji was contemplating, while having breakfast, what to do next. He remembered what he and the other villagers had a discussion the previous day. He quickly finished his breakfast and told Aysher who was still eating, 'Wait for me here, I will be back in a minute and walked away.'

As Aysher got up to keep his plate when Vaidji said, 'I have a surprise for you. Come with me.' 'We have thought that today I will come along with you and take you for a round, to all the departments. Later you can tell me which department interests you the most, and we can start from there.'

They both walked to all the sections of the village. They went to the food department to see how food was prepared on such a large scale, then they went to see how farming is done, Aysher even tried to sow the rice grains but his back started to pain. He also tried a hand at using the farming implements but it required a lot of effort. They walked to the cattle department but that didn't interest him much. They went to the weaving department where cloth was woven for the villagers. Aysher sat with the weavers and tried his hand at the loom for some time; this was the department where Aysher and Vaidji spent a little more time.

Later, they even went to the department where bamboo articles were made. They also had a small department where mattresses and beddings were made. They spent the whole day running from one department to another, hoping that this would create an interest in Aysher. But nothing concrete came out.

Chapter 14

*W*HEN IT was evening and it was time to go to the village, both Aysher and Vaidji went and sat by the river side. Vaidji wanted Aysher to choose a department but he had shown no keen interest in any of the departments. It was not just about working in a department, but to find an aim. His life was directionless and working might help him create an interest. This was a real reason for concern.

Vaidji said nothing. He just waited for Aysher to say something. 'I appreciate the way the villagers work in all the departments. It is something which you would not find in the cities. How are the villagers so hardworking Vaidji, how are they so dedicated?' But Vaidji sat unmoved still looking at the ground. After a pause Vaidji said, 'Aysher, we spent the whole day trying to find you a direction in life. This is something serious. It is high time you realize this. This is all we villagers can do for you. We are just a group of villagers who lead a simple and less complicated life. We have certain rules, certain ways by which we live and we are trying to help you live by them. Frankly, I don't understand why you are so confused. Either stay here or else you are free to go back to your city life. Make a decision. Only you can help yourself,' he finished and was about to get up when Aysher caught hold of Vaidji's hand. 'Don't go Vaidji, I request you,' said Aysher and Vaidji again sat down.

'You are right, I am not taking a decision. I am puzzled. I don't know whether I should stay here or go back to the city. I think I need time to nurse myself. There is something that is missing...something that is calling me. The city life was not for me, this life in the village is good, but this is not for me either. It is difficult to imagine myself working in one department for my whole life. My place has changed Vaidji, but my thoughts have not. They are still in flux. I hope my words have not harmed you, but this is true,' said Aysher.

There was pin-drop silence for some time, only the sound of the water trickling at the river could be heard. 'Aysher,' said Vaidji, 'you need to find yourself. I think I can tell you of a place and even help you reach there. Are you interested?' Aysher jumped with excitement, 'Really Vaidji? Do you know of such a place? Please help me reach there. I will always be grateful to you.' His eyes were twinkling with joy and he started to splash the water with his feet dipped in the river. 'When can I reach that place? What is the way to that place, Vaidji?' he questioned.

'There is some information I would like to let you know. This particular place is called the 'Sacred Forest'. It is in the middle of the dense jungle, where nobody goes. Sometimes a seeker who wishes to stay alone, goes to those caves in the Sacred Forest. But this has a rule and one has to abide by it,' and Vaidji paused. 'What is the rule, Vaidji?' Aysher questioned. 'It is a tough one, do not be emotional while going there. I want you to be logical,' said Vaidji.

'The rule is that a person has to spend at least fifty-one days in confinement. He cannot come to the village in between, no matter what happens. Even if he is ill and dies in between, he cannot opt out of it before fifty-one days. If he comes back before fifty-one days, he is not accepted by the village. Actually, the villagers feel that when a person goes to the Sacred Forest he gives up his life to God. If he comes out of it safe, then he is taken into high esteem and if he dies, then we, villagers, believe that his sacrifice is accepted by the Almighty. We villagers only come to the rescue after fifty-one days. We supply some rice and potatoes for fifty-one days that can be cooked in the fire and boiled in the hot water streams which flow in the forest. When you are taken to the forest, you are taken with a cloth tied around your eyes so you cannot see the way. We will leave you in a cave and then after the villagers depart, you can open your eyes. This is the only help we do. There is also a caution that you have to take. The Sacred Forest is a pious place, you cannot pluck flowers or fruits from that forest. The sacred forest will itself provide you with the supplies you will require. Never pluck a fruit even if you are dying of starving. Your deeds in the forest will affect the villagers. If you do not abide by the rules, an ill omen will come over you and the village. This is a truth and we villagers have experienced it many times. So don't think that this is all just a story. One thing is sure, if you come out alive, there will be a purpose to your life, or if you die, you die in the arms of the Almighty,' Vaidji's voice choked by the time he completed his statement. He had developed a lot of affection for Aysher.

'Sacred Forest, I need an aim. I need to be alone as you said to know myself. Please help me do this, be my support. Please,' said Aysher.

'Ok, son. My blessings are always with you. I am going to the villagers to inform them that you want to go and stay in the Sacred Forest. I have to make some preparations and also ask the priest of the village to perform a prayer before you go to the forest, which is a ritual,' saying this, he went away.

Aysher thought, only his body and his soul will accompany him, everything else will be left behind. Life is really unpredictable. He had planned that after two or three years, he would launch his own channel, and here he was, instead of opening a channel, he was going into silence. 'Life!,' he exclaimed, and walked back to the village.

When he reached the village, all the villagers were staring at him. It was strange even for all them to believe that a non-resident would take such a bold step.

Vaidji was sitting with some villagers and Aysher walked towards them. Suddenly one of the villagers questioned Aysher, 'Why do you think our forefathers made such a custom?'

As Aysher remained silent, the villager continued, 'this was made so that a directionless person is sent to the most natural setting. We believe if he is destined, he will get a deep understanding of oneself.'

Aysher smiled, and said, 'I want to go to the forest as soon as possible,' looking at all the villagers.

'Then be it,' said an old man. 'When this young man is so eager to tread this path, we should support him in all the ways we can. There are some things that mend naturally. We should conduct a farewell prayer in the early hours of the morning and then leave him in the forest. Make preparations, this is the correct time, otherwise rains would start.'

It was Aysher's last evening in the village, Vaidji was sitting beside him. Aysher said, 'This little hut has given me so much love that I will always be grateful towards it, and will never be able to forget how it has protected me. It has been like a mother to me, Vaidji. I will miss this hut and you during my stay in the Sacred Forest.

'We all will miss you too, son. You know, before you came to the village, the people of the village sometimes used to feel that life in a city is better and some have even left the village thinking the same, but after the picture you have shown us, nobody dares to talk about leaving the village. They feel that they should be happy for what they have. I want to thank you for this, for keeping this village united,' replied Vaidji.

Aysher smiled and continued, 'We all play a part in each other's lives, you have played yours and I have played mine. Let's see what more is in store for us both, how long we have to be with each other,' He paused for a few seconds and said, 'When is the prayer, Vaidji?'

To which Vaidji replied, 'It's early in the morning, son. I hope you come out as the blessed one, I will pray for you,' Vaidji said like a concerning father.

Aysher could not sleep throughout the night. He was very excited.

The new journey was his. It was free from all restrictions, free from all doubts, from all rules. It was going to be an experience of a kind. How will the animal feel when it will be left out in the open alone? How would it feel to not see a human being for such a long time? How would he feel not being able to hear any human voice?

It was morning when Vaidji came to Aysher's hut, he looked sad and depressed. He came in and said after sitting beside

Aysher, 'I am not at all happy that you are leaving, I wanted to help you and now I feel that if anything bad happens to you...' 'Not at all Vaidji, you feel so because you care for me and love me, but nothing will happen to me. I will come out of the forest on the fifty first day, hopefully as a better person. You know I need peace. I am waiting for those long secluded hours where there is no one to disturb. There is no human sound to be heard. I am waiting for the time I will spend sitting doing nothing. This all will be a kind of a balm for my soul. If I don't get this I will go insane. So, you are not pushing me to death, you are helping me from turning mad', said Aysher and smiled.

Aysher handed him a small packet, 'These are my belongings, Vaidji. You take care of them till I am back.' Aysher also wanted to say that if he was not back, he could give them to the children to play with, but he didn't say those lines as they would upset him. It was time for the morning puja and breakfast, so they looked at each other realizing that after this, there would be a long break before they could sit like this.

It was time to go and they both got up. Vaidji held the packet of Aysher's belongings close to his chest. As Aysher went out of the hut, he turned and looked around, his heart was beating fast as if he was already missing his home, he had tears in his eyes which he quickly wiped. The ceremony on the platform temple was very simple. As soon as the ceremony finished, the villagers started the journey along with Aysher. It was a ritual to beat the drums as they went towards and came back from the dense forest so that no cries could deter the person going for seclusion.

After the ritual, the villagers made Aysher sit on a square bamboo stool, it had four wooden wheels and was tied to a rope so that it could be pulled. Then a cloth was tied around his eyes; the last thing Aysher saw before being blindfolded was Vaidji's face. As the beating of the drum started, they pulled the bamboo cart. Earlier, Aysher felt a bit amused on experiencing strange treatments but as time passed by, he felt uneasy. The sun rays were not burning his skin as they had entered into a dense forest, the smell of the surroundings made him even more uneasy. After walking for a few hours, the villagers stopped. Aysher wanted to say goodbye to them and see some familiar faces, but he was blindfaced. He was then escorted to the cave and made to sit. No one said anything, all he could hear was the beating of the drums. He waited for some indication to remove the cloth from his eyes but even after waiting for some minutes, he got none.

After listening to the sound of the drums carefully, Aysher realized that the sound seemed to have faded. Oh! God they were going away from him, leaving him alone in this jungle. What the hell was he doing? His whole life revolved in front of him in fraction of a second...it indeed was a perfect life. A perfect job, house, a great personality and to top it all, a loving girlfriend and what can one call a person who will leave all that just to land up to this jungle waiting for a lion to come and eat him up?

Aysher got up and without much thought, pulled the cloth off from his eyes, and took a few steps. He was standing at the entrance of a cave, it was pitch dark inside. That scared him a bit, and in front of him was a huge dense jungle. The wind was blowing very hard that evening. The sky had clouds and the moon was also not very clear. It was a perfect setting for a thunder storm.

Fear overpowered Aysher's mind and body; he started to tremble a bit. He tried to shout so that the villagers could come back but his voice was choked. When his voice finally came back, Aysher shouted for help. But he knew it was all in vain.

A shiver ran down his spine, this was maybe his last few hours before being eaten by a tiger or a lion. Tears started to trickle down his eyes. The cave which was to become his home for a few days, seemed like a mouth of a dragon with sharp teeth. Suddenly, there was a lightning which made Aysher see his surroundings, there was also loud thundering making Aysher feel as if a huge chunk of the sky had fallen on Earth with a thud sound, and this thud sound was so frightening that it shook the earth.

'God,' he shouted out loud, and ran to the nearest tree. It again thundered with the same intensity and with each thunder, it felt as if it was the end of Earth.

Then with one more strike in the sky, it started to pour. Aysher looked towards the cave which had his food and also was his shelter, but all that seemed fake. It seemed like a trap of the demon to eat him up. Again a clap of thunder! There seemed no escape today. Aysher tightly held the trunk of the tree and closed his eyes. The tree was his only support for life, his only hope to live. In the end, survival is what man does everything for, and this was Aysher's fight for survival. The thundering and the heavy rains continued, Aysher was sticking to the tree like a creeper. He didn't know when he fell asleep.

Aysher opened his eyes when the sun was already shining bright and clear. He was not used to sleeping for such long hours in the village. By this time, the villagers were already down to work after breakfast. Aysher tried to change his position and realized that his legs and hands were all numb. His feet had a few insect bites due to which that area had swollen up. He recalled the last night which was very scary and thought that maybe he had fainted. His clothes were damp and some parts had dried due to the bright sun.

He got up with the support of the tree he held on to the whole night, and looked around. It didn't made him feel as homely as his hut in the village, but still it was also not as scary as he thought it was in the night.

His home was the cave which stood in front of him. It still made him feel a bit scared but he had no other option. He walked towards the cave and was about to enter it when he doubted that there might be some animal in the hiding and he should check before entering. He picked up a dry branch and started banging it on the floor. He kept on beating for a long time, when he became sure that there was no animal inside, he picked up a stone and threw it inside the cave. This could have been dangerous if there would have been an animal inside because the animal could have got hurt and attacked. Aysher had some experience of the village and he was sure that there was no animal inside the cave and then only he threw the stone inside to be fully sure that the cave was safe.

After checking, he stepped inside the cave which felt cooler, he carefully moved forward taking one step at a time. He wanted to see the end of the cave. After taking a few more steps, he could not feel the end of the cave, it was pitch dark inside and he could not see anything. The only thing he could hear was the sound of the flowing water. The only option left was to light some wood. He moved back and came back to the entrance of the cave. Aysher's priority was to make the cave safe. There were still some clouds in the sky and it could rain any time, this time he was not willing to spend the night outside. He quickly came out of the cave and gathered some thin, dried wood that could catch fire quickly. Then he ignited the fire by the technique he learnt during the stay at the village. He took a piece of wood and went again at the entrance of the cave.

The cave was quite long; Aysher was inquisitive about the sound of the water that was coming. He carefully moved forward but to his surprise he had reached the end of the cave. The cave was safe and fully closed at the end, but that sound was still coming. Aysher carefully observed the cave's end, it was solid and made up of huge boulders. As he moved from one side to another, the sound of the water increased. On a closer observation, Aysher saw that there was a small stream inside the cave, the water was coming inside the cave in the form of drops which was continuous and it was also disappearing behind the rocks and that is why the cave was fully dry. This water can be collected for drinking, he thought.

The next task was to clean the cave. He again went out and brought in a stem with leaves—this was his broom which he was going to use. He cleaned his home, and looked around to find his bag and other belongings. He took out a blanket placed it on the floor near the fire, took out some raw potatoes and kept them inside the fire to roast. That was going to be his food for the day.

When all was done, he realized that his clothes were damp, he changed into dry clothes and spread the wet ones on the entrance of the cave to dry in the sun.

Next task was to arrange for drinking water. He went out of the cave to look for some big round leaves and some long ones.

He carefully chose the long leaves and placed it in between the rocks so that the water, which was dripping against the walls of the cave, could be collected. He then held the big round leaves in a way that it could become a kind of a bowl. He collected water in his vessel and drank it.

In a couple of hours, he had made his cave safe, and the fire was burning to scare away the animals. He had his bed ready. He had access to fresh water and his food; the roasted potatoes were right in front of him. These were all five-star facilities of a jungle.

After doing all this, there was nothing much that Aysher had to do. He sat at the entrance of the cave with his back against the cave wall. There was peace all around, the leaves moved as the wind passed through them. Time for him had stopped ticking, it stood still.

The atmosphere was relaxing. There was nothing he wanted to do or think. He just sat and watched the different kinds of trees that were surrounding the cave. He also slept for some time. When he got up, the sun was about to set. He collected some dry wood so that his fire kept burning the whole night. After sunset, it was pitch dark. He shifted his bed a little inside the cave for safety, ate his potatoes and lied down in his bed in the silence of the forest. This was the end of the first day at the jungle.

Chapter 15

*O*NE CAN never have a sound sleep at a new place. Aysher was restless the whole night. Adapting to the new place, and that too, a jungle was not normal and easy. Whenever he woke up in the night, he used to add some wood to the burning fire and also used to inspect his cave with the burning fire stick. Weird thoughts started to come to his mind, what if a fierce animal crept into the cave and attacked him? Aysher was never scared of ghosts, in fact, as a reporter he had been to haunted places to shoot. But that night, he became very frightened, what if all the ghosts in the jungle came together and killed him.

There was still an hour or two left for sunrise when Aysher sat upright. He added wood to the fire and inspected the security of the cave. He then collected some water from the stream and drank it. It was not easy to kill time when alone. It was also strange for him to be alone in the jungle. 'What if I am the only person left on the whole planet. What if I am the last human being surviving,' he thought. All his thoughts were scary…and a shiver ran down his spine.

There are two sides to every aspect. Aysher wanted to feel the positive aspect of being alone. He wanted to feel the peace; he wanted to find his aim. He wanted guidance from God for a particular direction in life. He wanted a transformation from a city lad to a villager and also wanted his heart and mind to change along.

Vice versa, he was experiencing all the negative sides. He was scared for his life. He was scared of ghosts. He was also having thoughts as the next moment would be his last.

Coming out of that frame of mind seemed difficult. No matter how hard he was trying, his thoughts zeroed on to the same things. Living in the village had taught him at least one thing and that was, being his own judge. That is why he was waiting for the sunrise, maybe that could help him in thinking positive things. But alas! There was no sign of the sun. He thought if it would have been a normal day in the city, then he would have gone out, watched TV, cooked, read some book or chatted with someone on the phone. If he would have been in the village, then he would simply have gone to the village platform to regain his energies or talked with Vaidji or played with the kids on the platform.

Here in the jungle, there was nothing to do. There was no distraction to his one track mind. He looked around in the hope to find something interesting to distract his mind but in vain. His situation was also very absurd; he was sitting in a rocky cave, on a blanket, with fire burning in front of him. It was pitch dark outside, even the insects were fast asleep. He hid his face in between his knees and tightly shut his eyes. Soon he heard an inner voice, 'if you give up now, you will find it difficult to survive. These thoughts will kill you and your life will be a waste.'

'No! No! My life will not be a waste,' his words reverberated in the forest for long and then, again there was pin-drop silence.

He realized that sound has a long-lasting effect.

He took two wooden sticks and started to beat them on the floor. He was trying to see how sound breaks the silence. The sound was not much but, the way the sticks struck against the hard rock, it gave Aysher some kind of relief. Aysher was striking on the floor in a rhythmic way. Up-hit! Up-hit! Up-hit!, but after some time the wooden sticks started to break and spoilt the rhythm. He kept them aside and picked up stones lying outside the cave and again started his song with the same rhythm.

Up-hit, Up-hit, the sound of the rocks was better than that of the sticks and it didn't even break. Each hit was scaring away the negative thoughts of ghosts and animals from his mind. Slowly, each hit started to match the rhythm of his body, his breathing, his heart and even his thinking. Each hit overcame fear, each hit made him aware of himself, each hit made him feel all his pains, all at the same time. Each hit made him feel as if his heart was bleeding. Each hit made him remember all the pain life had given him. Each hit reminded him of Risha, her love. Each hit was a chapter from his life. It was a lesson he had learnt and the hurt it gave him.

Aysher was in the same state of mind for long. It was a kind of a trance; he kept on beating the rocks. He was there, yet nowhere. Two and a half hours later, his ability to strike decreased. His hands became weak; his fingers which were numb. He was drenched in sweat and his hands were bruised all over. Aysher stopped, he saw that the sun was shining bright and the birds were sitting on the branches of trees. Aysher's night had come to an end.

The rocks had broken from the edges and the floor of the

cave also had a lot of strike marks. Pain always leaves a scar, even the hardest rock cannot get away with it, and then how was it possible that the heart would feel no pain when hurt?

The fire was about to extinguish, Aysher added some wood to it. He then shifted his blanket away from the fire towards the wall of the cave and sat taking its support. He was totally drained but something had left him, there was a vacuum inside. It was negativity that had left him.

Chapter 16

*A*YSHER SLEPT for a few hours, when he woke up, he leaned against the wall of the cave. When he got up, he realized that it was afternoon and he needed to eat something.

His hands were paining and were also swollen because of the over exertion they had gone through. The villagers had supplied Aysher with rice and potatoes that were enough for him to survive for fifty-one days. Vaidji had told him that to cook the rice he had to dip the rice in the hot water spring near the cave, but Aysher was feeling very tired and also he didn't know the way to the spring. So, he thought of eating only the potatoes. He kept a good quantity of potatoes in the fire for baking and waited.

The day was extremely hot; there was not even a single patch of cloud in the sky. Aysher could hear the sound of a few birds, maybe they were communicating about the weather with each other. Every human at one time or the other, wants to be like a bird, he thought. What if he was a beautiful, colourful, bird, with strong wings that could take him anywhere he wanted? Even across oceans... a smile came to his face. But, is the life of a bird easy? It also has got its share of sorrows.

Sorrow has left no one; it touches every one. Why is sorrow such an integral part of one's life? Do we create it? Or make situations for it to develop? Or is it some kind of an exam that God gives before passing us to the next standard? Some say, it is the repayment of the follies or sins one had made in his previous birth.

Each question can be argued and answered for years but still sorrow stays. Why? Sorrow can be reduced by letting it be. Let it stay as the other things. If sorrow becomes the centre of your being, it will rule. Let 'being' be the centre and let sorrow stay in its confinement.

'I have become quite philosophical,' he said to himself. Aysher wanted to see what role sorrow had played in his life and thought of using his old trick. He took out his diary divided a page into two, wrote sorrow in one part and happiness on the other.

Under sorrow, he wrote: parents, siblings, holidays with parents, gifts on birthdays, dinner in hotels. These were the things that made him desirous of a proper family which he longed for in his orphanage.

Under happiness, he wrote: education, job, friends who were with him in the orphanage. He remembered how they used to share clothes, food and toys. Later he bought a flat, a car and had a good bank balance. He had a loving and caring partner and good health. This list was long.

This showed that he had few sorrows, then why was he behaving like the saddest person on Earth? Was it his destiny that had brought him here?

He started to shout aloud, 'I am happy, I am happy, woo! I am happy,' he repeated. Aysher laughed at his foolishness, he was such a blessed person and still he was running away from all the blessings of God. There was nothing to say or to think. He had been a fool, if coming to the jungle was destiny then moving out of it was again destiny. He firmly decided to end his foolish phase and move out of the jungle where his love and life was.

He thought of going back to the village and bid them farewell before going to the city but the villagers were simple people. They believed in their customs, they would never approve of Aysher leaving the cave before fifty-one days. If I leave without informing them, they will come after fifty-one days and conclude that I am dead. In this way they will have fond memories of each other, he thought. Life is unpredictable; Aysher had never thought that he would leave the cave in such a way. Aysher became a bit sad as there was nothing that he had done for the villagers; instead he had given them pain. He was a person whom they wanted to save, lost the battle halfway.

That night the thunderstorm was very strong and the fire could not be ignited at the mouth of the cave. There were chances of rain but fire was very necessary as that would scare away all the animals. Aysher ignited the fire a little inside the cave. He sat beside it with his heart full of emotions; some of joy and some of sadness. He was eager to tell Risha and all his friends, the story of his journey and experiences. This journey had indeed taught him a lot.

Slowly the storm started to pick up its pace, the roaring of the thunderstorm increased. The wind blew notoriously breaking all barriers. The direction of the wind was towards the cave and it was adamant on extinguishing the fire. Aysher tried to protect the fire, but all his efforts went in vain. Ultimately, the fire got extinguished and he sat alone in a jungle full of animals without any company in pitch dark.

Aysher moved towards the end of the cave and held a long wooden stick in his hand for protection. The storm became fiercer. The lightning struck again and again. Rains in the cities bring pleasure and water logging, but rains in the forest bring death.

It took a lot of time for Aysher to ignite the fire again. He then dusted his blanket, spread it beside the fire and lied down. It had become his habit to look towards the sky and sleep but as there were no stars that day, he stared at ceiling of the cave. Lost in his own sweet world, he had no sleep in his eyes. After long, he realized that there was something written on the ceiling of the came. He took out a burning fire stick and brought it close to read. It said, 'Dearest Aysher, we still have time to meet. If you believe, I will give you a way. Never stop at a place for more than 10 days. Hope to meet you.'

His world came upside down; he was face to face with the unexpected. Who had written it? How did he know my name? How did he come here? He thought if he should follow the instructions or not?

Aysher could not believe his eyes. All the joy of going to the city which had engulfed his mind had settled. The turbulence which had brought him from the city to the jungle had again started.

'Should I believe? Do I believe? Believe? In what? On the writing in a cave? The writing has my name. How? This means the writer knows me? Is it a joke? Who had played it? Believe? On God? On destiny? Do I have a company in the forest? Have the villagers done this? Or has Vaidji done this?'

A single question had the power to shake a non-determined person. Aysher was thinking that he was doing something very extraordinary, living alone in the jungle. Something unique, and unique things are not easy. He also thought that he has changed, but he was the same old Aysher from inside, who could be shaken by a single question.

He was scared now. He was totally wrong. What will be his direction in the morning? Towards the city? To the village? Or to some unknown destination? He lay restless on the floor of the cave. If he went towards the city, Risha will be delighted. But, if he wanted to believe what the walls of the cave said, he will have to leave Risha alone after ten days and move ahead, which she will not agree to. If he went back to the village, and enquired about the writings on the wall, the villagers might not take it in the right sense. What if a bad omen falls on them?

Aysher still did not know what to do and was also tired of thinking. He realized that it was getting cold and the fire needed some wood to burn. As soon as the fire started to burn bright, it gave a relaxing heat to Aysher. The sky was clear and stars were twinkling, the forest was dense, dark and quiet. It was haunting.

Aysher hid his face inside his blanket and a feeling of safety presided over him. In minutes he fell asleep.

It was the sound of the leaves that woke him up. His head was paining due to heavy thinking. The question still remained 'do I believe this or not?' He said to himself, 'My dedication of months and the simple living had been of no use? If I wouldn't have believed, I wouldn't have reached this place, which proves that I do believe but I don't approve of it. My journey is still not complete, and it will not be until my thoughts are clear. Without clarity of thoughts, it is useless to go to Risha and the village. Maybe life has something more in store for me.'

Life for Aysher had taken a U-turn again. His path was still hazy and the journey was incomplete. It is usually said that one can follow his heart or his mind but actually when you are in the doldrums , one can actually not follow anything but walk through the journey called life. One gets no option but to take up the challenge that life gives.

Aysher was in a no-option situation. He could not go to Risha or to the village, he packed his bag, some potatoes and rice for further use. He kept the blanket on his shoulder and moved out of the cave. Accepting the challenge without thinking further, he walked, he turned and thanked the came that was once his home. He hoped to return one day and walked away.

It was a hot day but the shade of the trees made it easy for Aysher to walk. He had been used to walking in the village. He was indebted to the villagers who had taught him like his own parents. The thought of the villagers always brought a broad smile on his face. He always prayed for their wellbeing. He kept on walking. The forest had no specific walking trail, so he used his own logic to walk in the direction opposite to the village. On his way, he saw small waterfalls, beautiful butterflies fluttering here and there. Huge bee hives, different varieties of wild flowers, colourful birds, lots of nests. All this kept him engaged and entertained. Whenever he got tired, he used to sit, relax for some time and then again continue. On his way he found a hot water stream in which he cooked some rice and also dipped his feet. It was in the evening when he started to look for a place to spend the night. During the day's walk, he found many small caves but there were none to be seen in the evening. So, he decided to spend the night on a solid branch of a tree and burn a small fire under the tree to scare away the animals. The night was spent peacefully and he continued his journey at daybreak.

The jungle was dense and he was walking for the past two days which had made him tired, although his body had adjusted a lot but sleep deprivation was taking a toll over his body. It had been a long journey on foot. Aysher thought that he was lost in the jungle. He kept on moving using his instinct.

It was on the third day that a strange yet attractive smell caught his senses. He stood still, closed his eyes and focused on the smell. He was actually trying to guess the direction of the smell. He stood still focusing but could not get the direction of the smell. It was the smell of food mixed with the smell of wood being burned. As soon as he realized this, his feet started to move in the direction of the smell. He looked up so that he could see some fumes coming from the fire and locate the place, but due to the height of trees he was not able to see the smoke.

Aysher quickened his pace as he knew that a surprise awaited him. The jungle was dense, Aysher was tired but the feeling of having company excited him to an extent that he was literally running by now. He had forgotten all pain, his heart was pumping fast, and he was just a few steps away from confronting humans, or a human.

He saw something moving in front, could also see the smoke, there was something behind the tree, and suddenly he was facing a human being, a companion in the middle of nowhere.

All eyes exchanged quick questions, how? why? who? But both were grateful for having company, and both faces had smiles. They walked close to each other and didn't know how to start the conversation.

Chapter 17

𝒯HE STRANGER was the one who started the conversation, 'You look very tired, come and sit.' he said softly and in a concerned manner. He guided Aysher to sit on a rock by the fire and gave him water to drink. He occasionally stirred the contents of the vessel kept on the flame and also kept on looking at Aysher. The dwelling place of the stranger was a small patch of land which was surrounded by huge trees. It was quiet and peaceful there. The stranger had made a small bamboo hut for himself. It felt like heaven in a jungle.

The stranger was a man in his forties, he had a lean body, small eyes with big dark circles which made him look older than he actually was. He was slow in his actions but his presence had a positive aura. Aysher felt relaxed and safe in the presence of another human being. He was extremely tired but more than that, being lonely had tired him more. Company made him feel comfortable. Yet the question still remained why was this stranger living alone in this dense forest?

Aysher thought that maybe some extraordinary situation had brought the stranger here. And, both owed an explanation to each other, but still they remained quiet. The stranger was busy cooking and Aysher was too tired to narrate his story and needed some time to open up in front of a stranger. At the moment he didn't want to get into lots of whys and hows. He felt happy, relaxed and safe; feelings which he wanted to enjoy for the moment. Aysher saw that the stranger had finished cooking and was pouring the contents of the vessel in two small cups and walked towards Aysher.

'I was not expecting company and so the quantity is quite less,' he said while handing over a vessel of steaming hot liquid to Aysher. Aysher accepted the service with gratitude and made space on the rock to accommodate the stranger. 'No, the quantity is not less, cooked food is a delicacy in the jungle,' and they both laughed. The sound of two humans laughing in the dense jungle even made the birds flutter in confusion. Aysher sipped the liquid and said 'this is very tasty, even the smell is so good, which brought me here; what is it by the way?'

'It is the root of a wild plant that has been boiled with water. It is rich in vitamins and minerals,' he answered. 'You look tired. I suggest you sleep for some time till I cook some food sufficient for both of us.' Aysher was tired and there was no reason to doubt the stranger's idea. Man has the basic nature of insecurity which is difficult to overcome, but people who are aware of it do not let negative thoughts master their mind. Aysher thought of God, thanked Him for the company and before going inside the hut, took out the potatoes and rice he had carried in his bag, and gave it to the stranger.

As he gave the potatoes and rice to the stranger, he said, 'Thank you and this is all I have to share.' The stranger accepted it readily and smiled. Aysher went inside the bamboo hut which was smaller than his hut in the village but still it was sufficient to accommodate two people. Aysher spread his blanket on the floor opposite the bedding of the stranger and went off to sleep.

It was almost dusk when he got up. His body felt a bit heavy when he got up. He opened his eyes and found himself alone in that small hut. His feet felt a bit sticky as if something was stuck to it. He was still not fully awake, his eyes were half open and body felt soft, when a weird thought came to his mind. 'Am I in quick sand?' he sprang up only to feel, see and touch his feet. Mind is the fastest of all and when alone in the jungle, it only thinks of extreme and bad things. 'Thank God', I am safe,' he said to himself.

There was some kind of an ointment that was put on his feet; he took some in his hand to smell it, the paste was aromatic. Aysher slowly got up and stepped out of the hut, the fire was burning but the stranger was nowhere to be seen. The same pot was kept on fire but Aysher stayed away as he had less experience of cooking. He just sat on the rock and waited for the stranger.

The evening skies usually have the same sight of birds returning to their nests. They are in a flock and fly back to their homes after a long and tiring day. Aysher hoped to return to his home one day. His home was in the city and the way to it was unknown. Just then he heard some footsteps and saw the stranger coming back from somewhere. He kept aside the packets which he carried and went straight to Aysher.

'How do you feel now? Your feet were swollen and bruised, so I had applied some mud and herb mixture. I hope you feel relaxed,' he said inspecting Aysher's feet. 'I am overwhelmed by your gesture towards me, a complete stranger,' said Aysher. 'I am anxious to know about you and the reason why you stay in the jungle. I hope you will tell me your story after which,

I will narrate mine.'

The stranger got up and said, 'Let's have something and then we have the whole night to talk our hearts out to each other.' They both enjoyed the simple meal of potato and rice in each other's company and then sat by the side of the fire for a long storytelling session.

The fire was burning bright, the wind was blowing mildly, and it was a captivating atmosphere. Aysher felt that the stranger was indeed a gentle soul, but some unforeseen circumstances had brought him into such a situation. But one thing was sure, that life had been harsh on both.

Then the stranger started to narrate his life to Aysher, 'My name is Raghu, I was born in Silol village of Uttar Pradesh, bordering Bihar. My father was a farmer and my mother was a simple housewife. We were five brothers and sisters, amongst whom I was the eldest. My parents were illiterate and for this reason they wanted all of us to be educated. They had high expectations from me, as I was the eldest and had to set example for the other siblings. I was a sober and an introvert person. My routine was very simple, I used to attend school regularly, and after coming back from school, I used to help my father in the fields. In the evening, I used to teach my sisters and brothers and then do self-study late in the night. I dreamt for a good future and also worked hard for it. Life was simple for us but not so simple for our parents, who faced a lot of crises but never let it come in the way of our studies. Life went on like this for years. I gave my tenth standard examination and topped in my district. The next day my name was in all the newspapers. This was indeed a proud moment for my parents.'
Aysher was listening patiently as Raghu spoke.

'Next, I took admission in class eleven and resumed my routine, but the incident of that day changed my whole life. That day, I had some problem in a particular maths chapter, so I stopped after school and took guidance from my teacher. After seeking the help of my teacher, I walked back from school, daydreaming about being a scientist and helping my father. Just then a speeding car stopped by my side and before I could think, they pulled me inside the car and sped away. Soon I realized that I was being kidnapped. They stuffed a cloth in my mouth and covered my eyes. From the way they were speaking, I knew they were locals and I was sure they had mistaken me for someone else. I thought that when they would know that I am a farmer's son who had nothing to offer, they would let me go. I calmed down and waited for them to open my mouth so that I could tell them my identity, but soon I lost my consciousness.' Aysher's anxiousness increased and he shifted closer to Raghu.

'When I got up, I saw myself lying on a bed, wearing shiny clothes and also saw a girl sitting on the bed, also wearing equally shiny clothes. The room was decorated, and as I tried to get up, I felt giddy and hazy. My eyes were itchy and my head ached. Everything seemed like a jigsaw puzzle.

The girl brought me a glass of water and smiled. I was totally confused but accepted the water. It was the first instance that I was alone with a girl, and after this realization, I tried to be at my best behaviour. After having water I questioned, 'Who are you and where am I? Who brought me here? Why?' Then I got up and banged the door which was latched from outside. I even shouted a few times, "I want to go home, please let me go," but there came no reply.' Aysher became more excited as the story proceeded.

Raghu continued, 'I sat on the floor leaning by the door, waiting for all the answers, confused and ill. After some time the girl came towards me and sat beside me. I looked at her, she smiled and unknowingly I also smiled back. Our eyes met, she was indeed beautiful. I was mesmerized and the questions in my mind faded.

She was dusky and had a captivating smile, big eyes and long hair. She stroked my hair and tidied them with her fingers. My headache vanished and I could not believe that I was so close to a female. Then she said, 'My name is Soni, and we are now husband and wife. My brothers had abducted you so that they could marry me off to you. They came to know that you are a sober person and also that you have passed class ten as a topper. Seeing a bright future, they married me to you as I am their only sister.' I was stupefied, 'You are my wife? Really? But how? When did we marry? I don't even know you? Where is my family?' I said.

Aysher was listening to the whole story in zapped attention, Raghu stopped to sip some water and then again continued, 'It was only after almost three months that I was allowed to go and meet my parents. My wife had conceived and my in-laws allowed me to go and give them this news. Till then, I was given all facilities and my wife was also by my side, there was only one restriction. I was not allowed to step out of the house.

My life had changed. My studies were left far behind and the other activities took the front seat. After staying with my in-laws, I had come to know that they were criminals; they all had been to jail sometime or the other. But I was bound by the love of my wife. My in-laws were mysterious people, they used to stay indoors during daytime and go out at night. Sometimes they were out for days. Whenever I tried to convince my wife to move out and start a separate life, she ignored my requests. She was allowed to go out of the house and whenever she used to go, she always came late.

One day, I was allowed to go to my parents' place, I was very happy. I thought that my parents would be delighted to hear that they are about to become grandparents. I pressurised my wife to come along but she gave excuses and said that she would follow later. My brother in-law dropped me outside my village from where I walked to my house. I knocked impatiently at the door hoping to see my mother but as the door opened, I saw a strange face standing in front of me.

'Who are you? Where is my mother?' I said sternly. Then pushing the lady aside I said, 'I am Raghu! Move out of my way.' I entered the inner area of the house calling, 'Mother, Father, where are you?' I called them several times but the air of the house seemed different. All the members of the house had gathered, they looked towards me with strange eyes.

The lady who opened the door stepped forward and said in a loud voice, 'Oh! So you are Raghu! Because of you your parents had to leave their house and fields at this age. Your parents have sold the fields and the house to us. You were such a good boy, why the hell did you want to marry that girl. She had many boyfriends. Who will marry your sisters when you are related to that criminal family?'

'The whole puzzle was solved, tears start to roll down from my eyes. I understood the whole situation, my parents had been misguided. They had been convinced that I had eloped to marry the girl and, they being innocent, fell into the trap. Fearing for the future of my siblings, they sold everything and went to an unknown destination. I sat on the floor and sobbed bitterly but there was no one to console.'

'This made me furious and on reaching my in-laws' place, I created a scene but they convinced me by saying that they were also trying to find my parents and their intention was not to break a family. Their main motto was to find a good groom for their sister and nothing more. They said that they were also worried of what had happened. All the reasoning was enough to calm me down as I have always been sober by nature.'

'Days passed and I had no work but to sit and listen to their criminal plans. Sometimes, I also gave suggestions which impressed them. I never went with them but slowly I became their mastermind. I drifted along as a leaf in the strong winds. They started to respect me and also depend on me. They even presented me with a gun, which gave me immense pride. My focus drifted from my wife, she also started to spend most of the time out of the house.'

'We planned to loot a bank one day, this was going to be our biggest loot. It took us days to finalize the plan and this time I was also part of the plan. Finally, the day arrived and we also became successful in looting the bank, but while we were running we were chased by the police. There was gunfire from both the sides and also causalities. I also fired a few shots, and in the end, me and my brother in-law were the only ones who were left and we ran away with all the cash on a motorbike. My brother in-law was sitting behind and I was driving. After some time, my brother in-law got hit with a bullet and we jumped into the river. He was badly hit and could not survive. I was a bit hurt and so I ran away with the money bag into the dense forest.

I stayed hidden for days and on enquiry, found out that all my in-laws had died in police encounter, the women of the family were sent to jail and then released later. My wife aborted the baby and married her lover. I tried to locate her, but it was all useless.'

'Destiny destroyed both my houses and my family. I am disowned by all and only loved by this jungle,' Raghu broke down after narrating his tragic life.

Aysher took a deep breath and said, 'We are all slaves to our situations.'

They kept talking for hours, later in the night Aysher also narrated his story.

They were two strangers, in a strange place and situation, sharing their life stories.

Aysher's stranger, now known to him as Raghu, had been through a roller-coaster ride in life and now he slept beside Aysher. There was still time for sunrise when Aysher got up. He looked at his companion, who had been a slave to his circumstances but at least he was aware of it. 'What about me?,' thought Aysher. 'I have not been a slave to circumstances rather I have jumped into circumstances. But why?' Raghu and Aysher were together in the same place; one knew the answers to all his questions, and the other still had to find them.

They both got up and after finishing their morning chores, lit the fire and made food. After some time Raghu said, 'I am going for work, you please take rest and I will be back by the afternoon.' 'Work?' said Aysher surprisingly. 'Not exactly, come along. Hope you will enjoy it too,' replied Raghu and signalled Aysher to follow.

Aysher followed Raghu as they both walked in the dense

forest trail. The leaves still had dew on them. 'We are about to reach my workplace, I hope you will not call me crazy after you reach there' said Raghu smilingly. Aysher was anxious to see the next surprise that Raghu was going to reveal. After a little walk, Aysher and Raghu reached a place which was quite rocky. The rocks were exposed due to lack of soil. The trees growing there were few and tall.

'This is my garden,' declared Raghu extending his arms. 'All these trees have been planted and taken care of by me. I love my work. The villagers are poor people and they need wood for cooking purposes, they come to the forest and cut wood, I plant them to maintain the balance. This huge forest had many such patches. This is my third such patch. Sometimes some villagers come and provide me with some rice and pulses.' Aysher was spellbound, he had no words. This was surely a big surprise, he had not thought that Raghu would show him this. Aysher was surprised, as how a young boy with high dreams had once become a criminal, and now had evolved into such a wonderful human. Raghu came closer to him and sat with him. They both looked at a small neem tree that was defying failure and was preaching positivism and success. 'This tree is just one month old and is very good for the atmosphere,' said Raghu. Aysher was still gathering his senses. He found it difficult to relate to the two different Raghus he knew.

After some time Aysher said, 'How did you think of such a noble deed? I am short of words, it's totally difficult to relate.' Raghu smiled at Aysher's question and said, 'My dear friend, you forgot the starting of my story. I am a farmer's son and since childhood I have seen my parents plant trees, but there is one more reason to it. I want to wash away all my sins so that in my next life, I am not made a slave of circumstances.'

They both sat for some time, and then engrossed themselves in planting the trees. Aysher enjoyed planting the trees and felt a sense of satisfaction. Aysher had told Raghu all about himself and even asked Raghu for his advice on the 'cave message'. Raghu was not sure about his own advice but he said one thing to Aysher, 'there are some good souls, and sometimes the lucky ones get guidance from them.' Both Aysher and Raghu lived with each other like brothers and time passed quickly.

It was on the tenth day that Aysher had to leave that place but before that they both had long and enriching discussions on various topics. Parting with a dear companion is difficult for all, Raghu wanted to accompany Aysher and nothing could be more suitable than that, but the police was still after Raghu. He had already left the money at the bank's doorstep but during the bank robbery, three policeman were killed. As for Aysher, he had by now become a wanderer by choice.

The morning that Aysher was about to leave, Raghu gave him a departing gift—a pouch full of seeds and said, 'My dear Aysher, you are my best friend and it would be a pleasure to spend some more days with you, but as we both know, each person has to tread his own path in the journey called life. I wish you all the best.' He handed over the seeds to Aysher and said, 'Promise me that you will continue planting trees always, this is something that will connect us like brothers,' his throat choked and they both hugged each other.

Aysher was accompanied by Raghu till the jungle's border and from there Aysher walked with quick steps towards the nearby village. Aysher took small breaks and continued his journey, he even walked during the night. He wanted to make the most of the time before making a halt of five days and also before getting tired. He walked for four days resting for just a few hours. Each time he thought of Raghu, he wanted to go and spend the rest of his life with him. But there was something that was pushing him to move, to wander, to seek, to search, and to achieve. He slept wherever he could find a place and then woke up and walked. He knew that if he stopped somewhere near the jungle, he would be tempted to go to Raghu. When his seeds finished, he bought some more and continued planting them, committing to the promise made to his friend and brother, Raghu.

Walking continuously had made Aysher's legs stronger, he had also started using a stick to walk as it made his walk much easier. His body was all tanned and lean. Procuring food was never a problem as the villagers had always been very kind and also his appetite had decreased.

Chapter 18

AYSHER HAD walked for almost five days, taking only hourly breaks and now his body badly needed rest. He had created a distance of a few hundred kilometres between himself and Raghu, so there was no chance that he could go back. His body had become very tired and weak, due to irregular sleep and tiresome walking. The food that was supplied to him by the villagers was not sufficient for his body. It was evening when Aysher saw an enchanting statue of a deity inside a shrine. The statue captivated him and he climbed a few steps of the shrine and sat.

After sitting there for some time, a voice distracted him, it was of the temple priest who was offering him some prasad. The voice of the priest was very gentle, he saw that Aysher liked the prasad and offered him enough to satiate his hunger. He also gave him some water. What more can a traveller wish? The veranda of the temple was huge where Aysher could rest, and also there was an easy availability of food. Aysher felt relieved. When Aysher came to the temple, it was crowded but later it became quite empty. The constant smile of the deity was what attracted Aysher and he kept on looking at Him.

Later Aysher was joined by the priest again, 'Here is some

more prasad for you, son,' he said while offering him some more. 'You seem to like the statue of the deity?' he said while sitting near him. Aysher looked at him and said, 'Aysher, you can call me Aysher,' he kept the prasad to one side and continued, 'the statue is indeed beautiful but what attracts me most is the smile of the deity.'

'Yes,' said the priest with a sigh, 'He keeps smiling at us but it is difficult for us to smile back.' Aysher nodded in affirmation, 'You are right Panditji, but why is it difficult for us to smile back? It is a simple thing to do, look I am smiling,' he said munching the prasad. 'This prasad is delicious, how is it made? This makes me smile,' Aysher said changing the topic.

The priest said smilingly, 'That is simple, but that's not the answer,' the priest moved closer to Aysher and now both were facing the deity, 'I have been a priest in this temple for years. I have been coming to this temple as a child, my forefathers have been priests in this temple. I have seen people coming to this temple and requesting God for all sorts of blessings. Later, some wishes are fulfilled and some are not. But the smile remained constant. Why?'

'I don't know much Panditji, but a father would always smile at his children, even if they have dirtied themselves in the mud,' replied Aysher. 'Then why do we suffer?' questioned Panditji. Aysher looked up, pondering over the question and then turned his head towards Panditji to answer, 'I think we suffer because of our own follies. Initially, we humans had a simple lifestyle, and we made shelters, grew and collected food and stayed in small groups. In those times we were happy, maybe even the creator was happy with His creation. We worked to fulfil our daily requirements and rested and relaxed in the left over time.

But strangely, our desires started to grow, they increased beyond limits, and to fulfil the limitless desires, we started to work hard. This hard work slowly took over our mind, we even desire for things possessed by someone else,' said Aysher laughingly. 'Imagine, we don't even use our mind that the other person's life and our life are not the same, even the lives of twins do not follow the same pattern. We act like machines. We never calculate how long we should work in life and then what should be done to relax ourselves. I have seen people on holidays, continuously managing their office.'

Panditji was listening but still was not much convinced 'I know this but...' Aysher interrupted, 'you must have seen people having a lot of cars, houses, bank balance, right?' he questioned Panditji. 'Yes, I have', responded Panditji in affirmation. 'But do you think a person needs to have three to four houses, lands, more money than his requirement?' Now panditji was listening. 'To possess so many things, we work more than a machine, this takes our health away. Still we are not bothered, but when there are less chances of our recovery, we at last climb the steps of the house of God.'

This is when God smiles and says, 'My child, I gave you everything you wanted, but what can I do when you are only asking me for materialistic things which later harm you.'

'I totally agree with you Aysher, I know of a gentleman who used to come to the temple and helped me a lot in getting the temple constructed, God gave him everything he asked for. His business grew and he became a millionaire. When he grew old, his children took over his business, and then the twist came. They started to fight over the possession of the wealth. His wife died of the shock, he was also left in an old age home by his children and later he also died. Sad, but true,' narrated Panditji.

They both looked at each other, Aysher replied in a sad voice, 'But still we humans indulge in this mad race which takes us to a dead end.' 'How do you know this? Who are you?' Panditji asked Aysher. He then continued, 'As you seem to know a lot of things, I have one more question for you. Why am I not happy with my life? I am the main priest of the temple, I perform all my duties. My father was also the temple priest here. My sons are also trained in this, and will continue the legacy after me. I have a small family and our life is happy and peaceful. My house expenses are taken care of by the trust, and we are happy with what we get. I never ask the devotees anything, still I am not satisfied.'

'You are a gentle soul Panditji, that is why the prasad made by you is so tasty. But I am not a learned man, I am also a seeker like you who is wandering in search of his answers,' said Aysher.

'Right you are, it is already time to close the temple. Would you like to come to my place?' he asked Aysher. He didn't accept the offer and said, 'I am grateful to you, but I will be more grateful if you allow me to rest in the temple for the night.' 'This place belongs to God and all his children are welcome here, I will give you a blanket and water,' Panditji said with concern.

Panditji made some arrangements for Aysher and left. He met a lot of people daily, but Aysher left a mark. While walking back to his house, Panditji turned to see the stranger who seemed different.

The peace of the place was infectious, the temple was surrounded by a lot of trees and the town was just at a walking distance from the temple. Aysher kept sitting on the steps and wondered about the smile of the deity. He was trying to interpret the meaning of the smile in his life.

Long after Panditji left, Aysher lied down on his blanket and used the blanket given by the priest to cover himself. It was a mildly cold night and the stars could be seen clearly they were shining occasionally as if dancing on someone's tune. The wind was smooth and brought along the smell of wild flowers.

Aysher was no more scared of the dark or loneliness. He rather enjoyed the peace where even he could hear his heartbeat. The sound of the vehicles bothered him, he had learnt to live alone. All the bondages that could tie a person were broken by him, he was free.

Each morning Aysher woke up with a peaceful mind. There were no thoughts in it. His stress had all fallen behind. Rather he was waiting for all the new experiences coming his way. He was in no hurry and knew that things would come at the appropriate time. Each moment, had now become important for him. Now, he needed no reason to smile.

He heard the steps of the priest much before dawn when he went inside to start his daily duties. Aysher looked towards the deity and prayed for more guidance. He then observed the sunrise from behind the trees, picked up his bag and went for his morning walk which included planting some seeds. Aysher continued his work till the sun was high in the sky. While walking back he could hear the temple bells at regular intervals.

'I thought you were gone,' said a voice from behind. Aysher turned and saw the priest standing behind with some prasad. Aysher smiled, took the prasad and said, 'Where can a person run from this enchanting place? I just went for my morning walk, which I continue till it gets hot.' 'I have got lunch for both of us today, we will have it together when the temple closes for the afternoon,' said the priest in a sweet voice and left to continue his duty.

Aysher kept on sitting and observing the people. Some came with their families and some came alone. Some were reciting some mantras and some were attending to phone calls. Each one had a different activity, no two were the same. But the deity kept on smiling in the same manner. Panditji kept on attending to all equally and when it was time for the temple to be shut for the afternoon, he came and sat beside Aysher.

'It is a very hot day!', he said while spreading the lunch. 'The food is simple, just a dry vegetable and some chapattis. This what I eat, hope you like it,' he said in a low voice. 'For me it is a luxury and it is better than any food that money can buy,' said Aysher. They both laughed and started to eat.

After finishing the food, both sat taking the support of the temple pillar, 'Tell me one thing, what makes you a wanderer?' the priest questioned Aysher.

'I will certainly tell you but you will think that I am crazy,' said Aysher. To which the priest replied, 'I have no doubt that if an educated person like you is wandering then he is crazy, but let me know the reason for the craziness,' and they both started to laugh.

'When you came in the morning to the temple I was awake, you got involved in your daily duties and I waited for the sunrise so that I could go and plant some seeds. This gives me happiness, on my way back I gave some portion of the prasad which you had given me yesterday to two kids who were playing nearby. I also saw a dog who was limping. I crushed some leaves and applied it on his wound, this gave me inner peace,' said Aysher.

The priest seemed a bit confused and said, 'Why do you plant trees? They grow on their own. We grow crops.'

'This is what I want to explain! Planting trees is not for my personal benefit, one day many people will benefit from the trees that I have planted today. This is my selfless service. I offered some prasad to the kids which I had saved for my breakfast, but then how could I have witnessed that smile which was similar to that of the deity. The planting of trees is a promise I have given to friend, this is my service to mankind.'

'I agree Aysher but all the seeds will not become trees,' said Panditji with concern. 'This is not what I think when I plant trees, I plant each seed with a hope that one day it would become a huge tree and provide shade, shelter and food to numerous others. My intentions are good and I pray to God to help me in my endeavour,' said Aysher explaining.

'But this is crazy! What do you do? How do you find shelter, feed yourself? This is extremely crazy! I thought you are a learned man,' said Panditji.

Aysher smilingly said, 'It is true that I am crazy, but little less than those who visit this temple for different desires and never for the love of God or to thank the Almighty for what He already has given. I am a little less crazy for sure. Let's talk about something else otherwise...' Aysher stopped lowering his head.

'No, no please continue, I want to listen, whatever it is. Let's see what you have in your mind,' said Panditji inquisitively.

'Then listen', continued Aysher, 'I think even you are crazy, you have been serving this temple all your life, you have spent a major portion of your life here. You consider yourself a good person as you are not greedy. True! You are not greedy, you are a gentle soul. But you perform your duty, you are not serving here selflessly, you are not here for the love of God. This is God's home and any such place is a centre of a lot of energy flow, haven't you ever felt so? If not why?' Aysher paused for a moment and then again continued, 'The other day you asked me, why you are not satisfied with life? I can answer that now. Try and see the smile that is on the face of the deity and serve people in a way so that you can see the same smile on the face of the visitors of the temple. This will make you complete, the link between God and you, is a selfless service to mankind. The void will become full.'

When Aysher finished, Panditji had tears in his eyes. He was spellbound, there was nothing he wanted to say or hear now. All that Aysher had said was true. He had only done his duty but never served God with love. A few minutes had brought a drastic change in his life.

'You are a gentle soul. I love your company, if any of my thought hurt you, please forgive me. These are some seeds, sow them, I hope it will give you some happiness,' said Aysher handing him over a packet of seeds. He then picked up his bag and continued his journey.

Panditji kept on sitting on the veranda and watched Aysher walk till he disappeared behind the trees. He then looked at the small seeds of hope he held in his hands. It was evening time when the temple had to be opened.

He wiped his tears and turned to open the door. He found his deity smiling at him and Panditji also smiled back with the same love and compassion which was brimming in his heart.

Chapter 19

𝓗ILL STATIONS have a lot of ashrams, while walking on this unknown journey Aysher came across many such ashrams. They provided him with food and shelter for the night, in this way they served Aysher. Aysher also developed a desire to give it a try, he wanted to experience life of an ashram, just to check if that was his true calling.

There were certain things that each ashram had and most importantly they all had a Guru. The students of all the ashrams were mostly foreigners. All wore a particular kind of a robe or a dress of a certain colour. But what attracted Aysher, was the communication that he could make with the Guru. So for days Aysher kept on searching for a suitable place, where he could spend some time. Aysher wanted to stay in a small ashram, when he went to big ashrams, he could not get a personalised treatment. It didn't seem like an ashram but more like a management school. So Aysher thought of searching for an ashram which was in a secluded place. This would make it less crowded because of its difficult approach.

Aysher started to move to higher grounds. The terrain was tough but the beauty of the places took away all his fatigue. After days of searching, he found the right kind of ashram.

This ashram's main branch was somewhere in the city and the Guruji of the ashram used to come to this place quite frequently. This ashram had all the qualities that Aysher wanted and so he got enrolled. The best asset of the ashram was the location, it was a picturesque place. The campus of the ashram was small yet beautiful, at a small distance from the ashram was a wild flowing stream. The gushing sound of the stream filled the whole atmosphere. The ashram had only fifteen to twenty members at that time and so Aysher got a whole room at his disposal. The room was scarcely furnished with just a bed and two chairs. The campus was managed by a lady, who was quite helpful. On the first day she took Aysher all over the place on her own, there she told him that she had also enrolled into the ashram after her husband's death and also had an eight-year-old daughter who stayed with her. She showed Aysher the small library that they maintained for reference purposes and also encouraged Aysher to continue his search.

The ashram made him feel safe as if he was in a protective environment. The walls sometimes made him feel safe and also sometimes restricted his freedom. The food was served in the common room near the kitchen and there Aysher was told that residents of the ashram help by offering free service to the ashram. The residents of the ashram used to work together and so Aysher readily took up the job of the gardener, his favourite area.

In a short time, Aysher adjusted to the atmosphere of the ashram. Right from the morning till the evening, Aysher made himself busy. He started his day with some yoga classes, then went for his gardening, then he had his breakfast and went straight to the library. The books in the library were very few but selective. There was a lot to contemplate on, after reading.

In the afternoon he helped in the serving of food since he could not cook, then he took a small nap. In the evening, he again went to his garden and after dinner he usually went and sat by the river side.

He was thoroughly enjoying his time. He was now eager to meet Guruji, and also had some questions in his mind. Timely food, sleep and rest was something that his body wanted since a long time. He became calmer from inside, it is in human nature to forget all about his past while coming in contact with new experiences. Reading was opening a new arena in front of him.

Aysher didn't have many friends at the ashram nor did he engage himself in friendly talks. He was rather involved in his own sweet world, which according to him needed much attention. But there was an exception, a small eight or nine-year-old girl was his friend, she was the daughter of the receptionist and Aysher used to help her in her studies, her name was Nandini. She was quite young but used to talk very intelligently.

The time Aysher used to sit by the river side peacefully, he felt heavenly. Slowly the frequency of his thoughts decreased and he became more and more composed. He used to gaze at the stars lying at the huge rocks. He could remember his childhood stories which said that his parents had become stars.

The stars had become his friends and companions, who said nothing, demanded nothing, promised nothing and taught nothing. They just stayed there and twinkled towards their friend who used to gaze at them sitting by the river side.

One morning Nandini came running to Aysher, 'Aysher, there is a good news. My mother had just received a phone call from the head office, Guruji will be coming to the ashram tomorrow for a two-day stay,' she exclaimed. Aysher became super excited, 'Thank you Nandini for this super good news, I hope I get all my answers!' he paused in hesitation. He then looked at Nandini and again said 'thank you.'

Nandini noticed this. 'Aysher you were saying something but then you looked at me and you paused, why? Do you also consider me a child?' she questioned. 'No my dear, it's not that, I am sorry if my act hurt you. I am just very eager to meet Guruji. I have already passed the limits of my stay here, after I meet Guruji, I will leave.'

'No Aysher, don't go, don't go please. My mother is so busy in her work of the ashram that she had no time for me. You help me in my studies and also I like to talk with you. No, you will not go,' she said stamping her feet. Aysher stopped his work and said, 'You are behaving as if I am going today, it's already time for your school and it's never good to be late. When you are back then we will talk, OK?' Aysher said changing the topic.

'OK, but don't go...' and Nandini left.

Aysher washed his hands and went straight to the reception to enquire. Due to the sudden plan of Guruji's travel, there was a lot to prepare. Everyone was on their toes, work was distributed amongst all the members. Everyone was very excited but the most excited member was Aysher.

That night while gazing at the starts he realized that each day would never be the same, but one should be stable and believe that the Almighty would do what is best and also knows what is best for His children.

The next morning the preparations at the ashram were on at full swing. Guruji was to come by 11 a.m., the organizing committee had made a very tight schedule—the welcome program, lunch, satsang, question and answer session, a small lecture by Guruji and also a small prize distribution programme had to be incorporated in the small time frame.

It was true that Aysher was super excited to meet Guruji and get the answers to all his questions but he also wanted to see what does a person who has devoted his whole life to the name of God look like. He had seen his picture in planners, posters, leaflets, pamphlets, badges, rings, lockets but that was not a substitute for a person.

When he was in the cave, he read the inscription of the wall, which said that he had to stay in a place for not more than ten days. Aysher had tried to follow the instructions as if they were the instructions of his own Guru. But he had not been lucky enough to meet his Guru, while at the ashram he had had the opportunity to read a lot of biographies and autobiographies. All the saints had followed the path of salvation that suited them or that was told by their Guru. Aysher was excited that from now on, he would also have a path in life where there would be no more questions.

The time of Guruji's arrival was coming closer, the ashram became the centre of a lot of activity, and the receptionist was keeping a tab on all. Slowly the news of some change in the program started to pour in. They were not confirmed and that increased the confusion, but the members kept preparing. Because the arrival was being delayed, the programme was also being cut short and last minute changes were made. The clock kept on ticking and there was total silence from the headquarters. This was saddening and took away all the excitement. Soon the members got distributed into small groups and started to waste time in futile discussion just to kill boredom.

Soon an official fax was received that the program for today is being postponed due to some circumstances.

Aysher went to his garden and started to plough the soil, but inside he felt restless. His mind was not at peace. He had put a lot on stake just on one thing, there was no other way out. He started to trim his plants with a heavy heart. Each day was challenging him. He heard someone calling him and as he turned, he saw Nandini standing with her notebook in her hand.

'Oh! You are here, I was searching for you all over the place,' she said and sat beside Aysher. The facial expressions of Nandini and Aysher were opposite. Aysher was sad as if he had suffered a loss and Nandini was hopeful that the solution to the problem was sitting in front of her.

Aysher looked towards her innocent face and tried to smile which seemed difficult and then continued to work. 'What is the matter, Aysher?' she questioned. 'You cook sad. I just want a little help from you in my homework,' she said and kept on sitting by his side while Aysher continued his work. First he was making a hollow in the soil bed and then planted the sapling of the seasonal flower in it. He kept on planting and she waited for him.

Aysher knew she was waiting but he chose to be quiet and continued his work. She had already asked him a question and was waiting for the answer. Wrinkles filled his forehead and at last he answered, 'I am sad because Guruji has not yet come, he could answer all my questions! I was very eager to meet him.'

Nandini started to laugh, 'You are so sad because you are unable to meet him. Is it the end of the world that you have come to, you can easily go to the headquarters and meet him there! It's true you will not get your own time but still you can meet him. But why so worried? OK, let's play a game. You ask me questions and imagine that I am Guruji, close your eyes, don't think but shoot.'

Aysher looked at the way she was convincing him and said, 'Nandini let's do your homework, show me your copy. These are bigger things and no kids play.' His rude words made her quiet and she controlled her tears. She bent her face, with all her hair falling over her face. Aysher realized that he had been too frank and she was just a kid. 'Sorry Nandini, I have hurt you, I am sorry, I didn't mean so.'

Nandini looked at Aysher and said in a strong voice, 'You know Aysher, you need to water the saplings you have just sown. You need to come out of your predefined notions that a person like Guruji can answer all questions. Are you sure the answers will guide you? They might even confuse you. Why can't you guide yourself? I simply don't understand the concept of people leaving their normal life, breaking all relations and coming and living in the ashrams. People break relations with their relatives to establish new relations of guru and disciple. Then you also leave all your responsibilities to get new ones. Are you people sure that you will be able to do justice to the new responsibilities? Why do you need a cage to live? Be like a bird in the sky, feel free, spread your wings, do as your heart says, be your own friend, do justice to yourself. Help yourself and be your own guide. Don't ask for help. You don't need it, you are a part of the Almighty, and how can the Almighty ask for help?'

She slowly got up and went away. Aysher smiled as this was not expected from her. His concept became somewhat clear, he watered the plants and went straight to his room. It was already time to leave the ashram. He packed his bag, completed all the formalities and before leaving the ashram, he made a small board in the name of Nandini and placed it in the garden, the 'Nandini Garden.'

Chapter 20

❧

$\mathcal{I}$T WAS pitch dark and was raining heavily but his eyes could see everything clearly. The saying on the cave wall came to be true. Now, Aysher had started to believe in destiny, in God, in life, in his deeds, everything. He had now understood that destiny had brought him from the city to the village and then he became a wanderer. No one would believe the reality that, a little girl who herself needed help in doing her homework had shown him the way. It takes a lot of time for one to understand his destiny and when he knows, there is no looking back. His path was a little clearer.

He was now heading towards the cave where he read the instruction on the wall, to meet his guide. Aysher believed no matter what the difficulties are, he would wait for him and he will definitely come to guide him, enough of wandering without a purpose. He was not a wanderer now but a disciple of his guru, without even knowing his guru. He started his mental prayers while walking.

Aysher kept on walking for an hour or two. He was not bothered about the rains or that he was drenched. He had only one aim and that was to meet his guide.

Aysher had heard stories about saints who live in caves and

also read about them while in the ashram. He knew that the saints purposely keep themselves hidden from people so that there can be no interruption in their spiritual journey. Aysher walked briskly as he wanted to cover more distance in a short time. He felt excited as he was about to meet the unknown person who knew all about him.

Thoughts that make one happy are the ones a person likes to think repeatedly. Happy thoughts are like sweet juice that act as an antidote to a heavy heart. Aysher noticed that the rain was becoming stronger and stronger and it seemed that the rain God was up to something, but he was so engrossed in his own sweet world and kept moving.

Aysher continued to walk, he crossed two villages, a town when he started feeling the need for some rest. No doubt the life of a wanderer had taught him to walk for hours without food, water and rest, but he was still a human being. He started to look for a place where he could have some tea and snacks. He had walked almost the whole night, the sun was about to rise and Aysher heard the sound of the train, he realized he was near a railway station and moved in its direction.

Far away, he could hear some sounds and he headed towards it. He saw a few people gathered in front of a small shop. As he moved closer, he saw the people were totally hooked to the TV screen.

There was breaking news being flashed on the TV screen, 'UTTARAKHAND UNDER FLOODS,' and the screen showed how water was destroying all that came in its way. Buildings were being smashed by the strength of the water, cars were swimming in the water, reports were still coming in and number of lives lost was still unknown. A massive cloudburst that had triggered this tragic incident, this had also caused lots of landslides. The news didn't say much about the loss of life but thousands were stranded in the area. There was total commotion. Aysher felt concerned and sorry for the ones who had lost their lives.

After some time he ordered a tea and a few biscuits and took a seat on the bench. If he would have been in the news channel, he would have rushed to the place and covered the incident as much as possible. Today, he was at the other side of the screen. This was his choice and his destiny. It was now more difficult to reach the cave but he was determined. His tea was served, he took the hot tea in his hands and took a sip.

Slowly, more and more news started to pour in. Aysher was about to finish his tea when the news channel started to flash the name of the places where the tragedy had struck the most. His ears heard a name and his eyes got transfixed to the screen. Now, no sound reached his ears, he was not able to believe, he took the support of the wall to stand and confirm the name. The centre of the cloud burst was too close to his village, Phulma, the village of Vaidji. He thought, 'Oh! My beloved village, how are the people? How can I help in this tragic time? This time I will also help them rebuild the village? What if I was in the cave? I would have died! I hope Raghu is alright.' All sorts of thoughts were hitting his head. This has been so sudden. This is the second time that such a tragedy had struck the village. His main concern was the wellbeing of his brothers and sisters. He hoped that they were all well.

Now, his main concern was to reach the village at the earliest. He had no time to waste and he should quickly make a move. He started to make enquiries about the ways he could reach the village. Some people gave him answers and some were themselves confused. One even questioned, 'Why do you want to risk your life? There is only death and devastation there.' But their comments could not shatter the determined thoughts of Aysher. He had to go to the village at any cost. He required a conveyance to reach quickly.

Soon Aysher was on his way towards the village. Destiny can make one do strange things. He had never thought that he would be walking towards the village in such a situation. It was still raining but Aysher was least concerned, he just kept walking. He kept on enquiring and walking. The hills that had enchanted him earlier, now seemed deadly, ready to engulf everything. The river was flowing in fury. On his way, he could see people removing water from their houses, some were trying to put sheets on top of the roofs to protect themselves from the rain. Some were leaving their homes to safe places. Some were crying, due to the loss of life and shelter. Some were searching for their loved ones. The catastrophic tragedy had affected all and Aysher was sure that the situation higher up would be worse.

On the second day, Aysher saw a van moving upwards, this was unusual because he had only seen downward movement. He ran behind it and it stopped. The driver was quick to offer him a seat and they moved towards the village.

Actually the driver was a resident of the village and had gone to the city to sell the handicrafts item that the villagers used to make. There was no conversation between both of them. When the road was blocked due to landslides, they waited, had tea and then again moved. The people also did not disturb them when they saw that the van was moving towards the centre of the flood.

The wait was endless. Every hour, every minute, every second counted. Both had tears in their eyes and hoped in their hearts for the well-being of their village. People had experienced all sort of losses. Each eye had been a witness to the fury of the Almighty's anger. One thing that came clear in front of everyone that no matter how advanced or developed we humans become, trying to search for the aliens, trying to make colonies on other planets, but we stand nowhere in front of the creator and the destroyer, the God.

We just survive on His love and mercy. The day He decides the end, we have no chance of survival. But the big question was, what should be done so that His mercy prevails on us. What will make Him happy? And suppose we know the answer, it is love.

Aysher and his companion were slowly but steadily reaching their destination. They both ate nothing and only survived on tea. Some didn't even charge them for the tea as a gesture of help.

We humans are strange; unless we are shaken from within, we never help. We want to be rewarded for everything. In normal times, the same people would have charged them double the amount for two cups of tea. Why do we forget to help? Why does God need to remind us? All eyes that met them on the way were questioning them, why were they heading towards the centre of the tragedy?

It was on the third day, that both the travellers were nearing the village. They were both extremely eager, the tears in their eyes had dried up and eagerness had filled all the corners of their heart, body and mind. When they were just five to six kilometres away, they reached a dead end. They both left the van and ran towards the east, but after half a kilometre, they found themselves atop a cliff and the river was flowing under it. They thought that maybe the floods have damaged the way. They moved towards the north and again faced the same situation. All they could see was a fierce and rugged river. They both looked at each other as after seeing the situation, their hearts were almost skipping beats. Tears started to flow from Aysher's eyes. He ran like a mad person towards the west, his companion refused to move and sat on the cliff wailing in agony of losing all. He had a better idea of the place and knew what could have happened. But as Aysher moved towards the west he saw the devastated forest in front of him. The trees were uprooted, huge logs of wood floated in the river. The river had receded but what it had left behind, was destruction and devastation. The trees had witnessed the calamity.

'Where is the village?' shouted Aysher. He looked back and saw his companion, crying. His mind started to calculate, he pointed at the directions to get the exact location but was unable to locate a thing. He ran towards his companion, who was better with the directions.

'My family? My kids? Why did I leave you alone? I should also have gone with you...take me with you,' the man cried. Aysher still hoped to locate the village. Tears were rolling down his eyes, and his hope was slowly decreasing.

Aysher shook him and questioned, 'Are you sure that we are in the right place? Think!' Aysher shook him again and looked into his eyes, 'Are you sure we are on the right path? Please answer me!' The companion stopped sobbing, there was tears all over his face, 'Aysher, I can walk from the city to the village and even blindfolded. This has been my route since the age of twenty-one, and now I am forty-nine.' He pointed towards the cliff, 'The village, our home has been washed away by the river that flows under the cliff.' Aysher ran towards the cliff again, only to find the rough river flow which spared no one. The river does not differentiate between good or bad people, it just destroys whatever comes in its way.

Aysher again became an orphan, the second hit is always harder than the first one. It was hard for him to believe that the whole village was washed away by the floods, and there was no sign of the remains, but it was a reality.

Chapter 21

Aysher turned around and walked away without saying a word to his fellow companion who was crying bitterly. He had totally lost it, the tragic sight had broken him, he felt miserable and he just walked away. Aysher's senses had gone blank, he had no thought in his mind and he just walked as that was the easiest thing he could have done. He was just a mass of flesh. His ship had capsized in the sea and it was up to the sea to take him anywhere it wishes.

His mind had withdrawn itself just like a tortoise who protects itself from external harm. He was walking as if a non-living person. He had turned into a stone which does not even feel the pain when kicked.

He kept on walking with no energy. But he kept on and on as if driven by a force. As if being pulled somewhere. The way on which he was walking was unknown to him, he was absent minded, but still kept walking as if he knew the way. There was nothing that could bother or hurt him. The rain, the cold, the sun, the thirst, the hunger, all became small in front of his sorrow and could not deter or stop him. Nothing can be done to a non-living thing.

He looked like a mad man, his bag was also left behind

in the van, his clothes unruly, his hair was unkempt, he had a rugged look, his eyes were dry and dead, his lips were parched, his shoes were all soiled.

He was slowly walking towards the peaks, it was becoming colder and chilly. But he was not feel it. One dark night, when Aysher was walking like a dead man, it started to snow. It snowed more and more and after some time, it became difficult to walk. Aysher was stuck in one place. He was slowly turning numb. First his feet, then his legs became numb, after that the numbness moved up and after some more time, it became difficult for him to walk. His heart beat slowed down, it seemed that they were the last few moments of his life. The candle of life was slowly withering away leaving behind its memories. Death was nearing and just when life was about to leave the body, someone interfered.

Some warm and loving hands held him and dragged him. He had lost all his consciousness due to a fever. But he could still feel the loving hands taking good care of him. It wasn't much that Aysher realized, but knew that his life was back. He survived.

It was after two days that he could properly open his eyes, as soon as he tried to get up, someone helped him to get up. He was given some water, Aysher saw that he was being taken care of by a young boy in his twenties. He was fair, with well combed hair, and he looked very pleasant. As Aysher kept the glass by the bed side, he smiled.

Aysher smiled back and nodded his head. 'You were about to die, how did you manage to walk to such a great height, without proper clothing, food and water? That too alone!', he exclaimed. Aysher signalled him to make him lie down. 'You are indeed a brave man, I cannot even think of such an adventure. You know when we reached for help, you were almost frozen, we had to pick you up just like a log of wood on our shoulders, and then we kept you very close to the fire and poured hot water so that the ice around you could melt. What an adventure!' He giggled, the innocence of his age was apparent in his talk.

'Oh, I am sorry I did not introduce myself, I am Hari,' he said. Aysher looked at him and said half-heartedly, 'Thank you for saving my life, Hari,' and took a deep breath.

He then closed his eyes and the thoughts again went to the tragic scenes that he had witnessed. Life was acting strange, he was saved two times. One year back, no one could imagine that Aysher would have had such experiences ahead. It is said that experiences make a person, they make the future, but what the hell were his experiences teaching him! He knew that Hari was sitting right by his side but to avoid a conversation, he kept his eyes closed. After some time, Hari went away and Aysher slept.

Aysher was feeling better now, the fever had subsided, and Hari again got some rice and pulses for him. Aysher ate it silently, thanked him again for his care and again closed his eyes to avoid a conversation. He did not want to come out of his shell. His shell was full of agony, pain, loss, heartbreak. He did not want to think of anything else. He was like a worm tied inside its own cocoon.

The next morning when Aysher got up, he was happy not to see anyone in the small wooden hut. There was bedding right in front of his bed and also a water jug. Aysher helped himself with some water. He opened one door and saw that it led to another room which was being used as a kitchen. It had just the basic things required for cooking. He then went towards the other door and opened it to see that it was white outside. Snow covered every inch of the ground and also the trees. It was quiet, peaceful and serene. Aysher started to feel cold so he closed the door and went to the window to open it. The window which was to the other side of the room also opened up to the same scenery. The scene was so beautiful that it did not let any negative thought come to his mind. Aysher touched the snow that was accumulated by the window—it was cold soft, fresh and white.

He could remember how in his childhood he used to love the ice that used to get accumulated in the freezer, and he used to use his hands to scratch it from the walls of the freezer and eat it, it tasted heavenly. Aysher unknowingly picked up the small piece and just when he was about to put it in his mouth, the door opened. Hari stepped in, Aysher turned and Hari saw him in the act. 'No! no!, don't do that, you are just up from fever,' and they both burst into peals of laughter. This was after a long time, that Aysher had laughed.

Seeing him laugh, Hari said, 'You should not let the smile vanish from your face, no matter what the circumstances.' 'True,' said Aysher 'but I am sure you would not say that if knew what I have been through.'

'Let's keep that for some other time, I went to get some supplies from the village. Come and help me in the kitchen,' said Hari changing the topic.

Hari brought with him a wave of freshness in Aysher's life. He was full of enthusiasm, he laughed. Aysher was loving his company. They spent the day cooking, cutting wood for fire, Aysher even went to sleep in the afternoon when Hari again went out for some work. It was in the night that they both sat in their beds near the burning fire and started chatting.

They were both talking about how Hari had brought him to the hut when Aysher was struck with a question. He questioned Hari, 'Who was with you when you brought me here?' Hari somehow wanted to avoid the question, but Aysher pestered him. Hari looked at him and smilingly answered, 'It was Guruji, we both are the students of the same Guru. That day, Guruji was sitting in meditation for the whole day and when he got up, and I offered him food. He instructed me to come along. It was snowing heavily and was pitch dark, after walking for about three kilometres, we found you stranded in the snow. Guruji was here for one day and he took care of you like his baby, the next day he handed me this letter and went away.'

Aysher could not believe his ears, he was shaking when Hari handed him an envelope on which it was written,

For my loving son, Aysher...

Aysher broke down with the loving words. All his pain got washed away in the pure words of love. He held the letter close to his heart and cried like a child. After a few minutes he felt better and opened the letter.

Dearest Aysher,

Hope you are feeling better now, my son. It is true that your life has given you a pretty hard time, but, my son, do not lose hope like this. There were very difficult times in your life but those were due to your own karmas in your present and previous life.

Now where you stand, your good and bad deeds are balanced. I can promise you, from today if you do not hurt

a single soul, you would never get hurt or feel the pain. You have no family, and destiny has kept you free from so many bondages. You have experienced life and death. You know the answers to many things because of your experience.

You have followed what I had said about travelling through the cave message, I knew that destiny will bring you to this hut and I wanted you to practice walking and experiencing life. Remember, you are like my son, I am walking a few steps before you. Just have faith, believe and continue your journey.

I know you are very heartbroken with the tragedy that had happened in the mountains lately. I am also very heartbroken but cannot do anything except pray to the Almighty. You have a bigger role and all that had happened in your life earlier, had happened for a reason. You have to make people aware that they have to live being a part of nature and not by destroying it. The balance has to be maintained, if it is not maintained, in this way the nature will balance itself with some more fearful calamities.

I also know that you are eager to meet me, we will meet but only when you are ready.

Hari has already made arrangements for you to go safely to the city. Go and meet Risha, she will be your companion in your and my dreams of a better world.

I love you my son, and I am always with you.

Your loving Guru.

The words were like an ointment. Aysher stared at the wall, he opened the window and felt the fresh air. He felt safe and he now had the answers to lots of his questions. He now had a goal in life and till now he was just being trained to fulfil it, and also paying for the follies he had committed in his previous and present birth. He smiled. His life was really unique, he was actually in search of his Guru, and was destined to meet him in this hut after all the previous experiences.

He felt lighter, he turned and saw Hari sleeping. The ice was still on the window and this time Hari was not there to interrupt him, he knew that his Guruji was watching. But like a child, he slipped some ice into his mouth and smiled at his mentor, who presumably was smiling back.

The next day, there was a continuous smile on Aysher's face. His path was clear, he had to fulfil the dreams of his Guru. He had to work on something at such a big scale that the whole human race could benefit from it. He was in a way surprised that Guruji knew about Risha and him, and was happy that she would be with him in his journey.

What was making him even happier, was that his frantic and direction less search had brought him to a goal. Now this was going to be his inspiration. He was ready to devote his life to this goal. Earlier, his path was unclear, he had a few ideas but he was too excited to think about all of them in detail. Things in his life had started to fall in place.

Later that day, Hari told him that a man will take him to the city on his motorbike and from there, he can catch a train to reach his home. They both had lots of time in hand and so Aysher told him about his journey. Much was, of course, known to him through Guruji, but not in such detail.

When asking about Hari, Aysher came to know that Hari had been rescued by Guruji when his whole family met an accident. He was the only one who survived, and he was very young when he landed in the safe and caring hands of Guruji. Hari was just six then. He could not tell much about himself and his family, and so there was no option left.

There was one similarity in both of them, both did not have biological parents with them, but have the loving guidance of their Guruji. Through the conversations, Aysher questioned, 'Hari, what do you think is the reason for Guruji not meeting me?'

'This is tricky,' he said, 'but I think, that he was waiting for the right time to meet you, maybe he feels that you are not ready? I might be wrong. You see brother, Guruji knows you in and out, and he knows why you were disturbed, what you want. What the future holds for you, he knows everything! He knows you like a creator. He knows your destiny, even your previous births, even before that. Trust me, I have been with Guruji all this time. He still amazes me.'

'True,' said Aysher 'but what do you think he wants me to do, that which will bring about a drastic change? How will I, with my already confused mind, think about it?' he paused then again started, 'don't you think it would have been better if he would have told me what he wanted. Isn't it?'

To this Hari answered, 'I am sorry. But I differ from you. You have to take your own path. There might be different ways to reach a particular place; you have your own reasons for your path and I have mine.'

'This is again true, brother. But I am feeling very happy to be with you, and it would have been great if we could spend some more time together. Don't you think so?' said Aysher looking at Hari.

Hari smiled at his innocent brother who had a long path to tread. 'You see Aysher, Guruji has already left for his meditation,

I also have to follow him. We are praying for the well-being of the human race, we are doing our bit in our own way, you have to do yours. There is no time, you must hurry and start your work.'

For some time there was silence in the room, Aysher knew he was behaving very casually. Aysher was behaving like a hungry child who was happy with just a cuddle, but he forgot hunger is a totally different thing. Aysher had known some answers, that made him happy, but there were bigger questions to be answered. People were dying for no fault of their own. Thousands had lost their lives and lakhs have lost their homes. This should not continue. This has to be brought to an end, and an even bigger reason to take things seriously. It was a huge responsibility.

The morning when Aysher was about to leave, he hugged Hari warmly. There were tears in both their eyes. Partings are always sad. As a parting gift, Hari gave Aysher a small blue flower, 'This, my brother, is a parting gift to you. I hope you are successful in all your work, I will always pray for you. Its fragrance will always remind you of me and your goal. Never lose hope, brother, God is with you.'

Aysher was touched. It took him three days to reach to his city where Risha was, but the flower did not shrivel and its fragrance remained the same. It was a blessing indeed from one brother to another.

Chapter 22

*A*FTER THREE nights, he rang the bell of his flat. The watchman was surprised to see him after so many months and the door still had his name plate. Everything indicated that Risha was still waiting.

And the door opened.

She stood in front of him; she was surprised, astonished, amazed, happy and pale all at the same time. Her prayers had been heard. Tears started to flow from both her eyes, she gently stepped forward and hugged him. No words were spoken, there was silence everywhere. No questions were asked nor were answers expected. Both had missed the other one, both had suffered a lot and now the presence of the other person was the only medicine that was required. Aysher gently squeezed his lady love in his arms, she was his strength, she was his love, she was his world and now there was no doubt about it.

Risha started crying even more bitterly, this made even Aysher cry. Aysher was overwhelmed by her love, devotion and her patience. She had suffered so much just for the sake of love; it was not what she deserved.

Aysher held Risha's face in both his hands and said, 'I am sorry, Risha. I am blessed to be loved in such a way.' Risha stared at him and just said, 'Aysher.' His name never sounded so sweet. They both stepped inside and closed the door.

Nothing in the house had changed. Risha was still holding him tightly as if he would run away. Aysher was in no hurry to tell her what all had happened in the past months. After some moments of silence, Risha stopped crying and looked up only to find that Aysher was in a mess—his hair was all unkempt, his clothes were dirty, his lips were all chapped. 'Where were you, how have you been, you look unwell, you have lost so much of weight! Still, you look at peace.' She said with a lot of concern in her voice.

'I will tell you everything but at the moment I am very hungry, and would love to clean up, after which I will tell you the whole story,' said Aysher.

'Oh! I am extremely sorry, I will quickly get you something, you go and freshen up,' and she quickly went towards the kitchen.

It had been months since he last cleaned up properly. The first thing he did, was he took out the flower his brother Hari had given him as a parting gift, and kept it on the table—it was still fresh and smelled wonderful. All this had to be told to Risha, and as per Guruji's instructions, her help was also required in his goal. He had to be quick; he went straight to the bathroom, and it indeed felt like a luxurious experience. He was now in a recognizable condition; when he came out, he was not surprised to see that Risha had already taken out his clothes for him. He quickly dressed up, looked at himself in the mirror and went straight to Risha.

After a long time that both of them were sitting on their favourite couch, cuddled up together. Aysher was still feeling bad that he had hurt such a gentle and delicate girl. She was a devoted person. Risha was caressing his hands, she was with him now and nothing else counted for her. She had already forgotten all the pain she had gone through. There were no questions in her mind.

After some time, Aysher broke the silence, 'Risha, don't you want to know what I was doing all this time?' she looked at him and answered, bringing his hands close to her cheeks, 'I have you, that is all that matters to me. You are my world,' and she smiled. It was a simple yet strong answer, which he had already expected.

'Risha,' he said, 'look at me, I want to share my experience with you, lend me your ears for some time. I know you are happy but my experiences were out of the world.'

And Aysher started to narrate his whole experience. Risha didn't even say a word in the middle, her eyes became wide open during the narration. Some incidents made her cry, some were scary, some were overwhelming and some made her jump in amazement. It was in the end that Aysher got up and kept the flower in Risha's hands. She shivered in amazement. After the narration, she had no words. She kept looking at the flower for a long time, she had never expected this kind of experience from life, this was certainly unexpected.

Life had been strange for both.

It was almost morning when the narration finished. Risha and Aysher were extremely tired, both went to sleep but before that Risha texted her boss saying she would take a leave of four days.

Aysher was extremely tired and so as soon as he went to bed, he fell asleep. But Risha was awake. She was trying to behave normal in front of Aysher but the truth was she was not feeling normal. It was still hard to believe that Aysher was sleeping right beside her. All these days, she was waiting for this day. Now when this day was finally here, she could not believe it.

Risha sat upright and closely observed her love lay curled up in the bed right next to her, his face seemed so calm. Risha also curled up close to him. Aysher was not facing Risha and so she gently kept both her hands on his back to feel his energy and his presence. Aysher was her sun and she was his Earth; she was lifeless without his energy.

Today after many days, she felt safe and protected. Earlier she used to sleep in fragments but today she would surely have a sound sleep. There was some kind of energy on the bed, it was warm with the warmth of her companion and love. She was still unaware what she should think about the experiences that Aysher had told her about, but one thing was sure, she would do whatever he would require of her.

Till the time they went to sleep, Aysher had only told Risha what had happened in his life, he was yet to show her the letter of Guruji. And about what he wanted to pursue. He was also waiting for the time to inform Risha that she had a major part in his aim to do something big for the well-being of the society.

There was still lots to unfold. In the following days, Aysher showed Risha the letter which had her name. She was not at all a difficult person to be convinced, as she wanted to be with Aysher in all his steps in life. But the question still remained, what should be done to benefit the maximum number of people.

Aysher and Risha usually donated to ashrams and trusts, but that work was on a very small scale. Opening an orphanage or an old age home or working for a special section of the society, was not their aim. By this time, Risha had put in her resignation, citing personal reasons. Both Aysher and Risha were constantly brain storming over what they could do. Their day would start with discussions, they would arrive at an idea which they would develop and then it would lead them to nowhere. Again, they would brain storm on another idea.

Three to four days went by in this same manner and no solid idea emerged, when suddenly a strange thing happened. Aysher started to develop a persistent headache. This diverted their attention; when a doctor was consulted, he cited a very strange cause for it. Aysher was suffering because of change of climate, and now his body was finding it difficult to live in such enclosed and polluted environment.

This made Risha and Aysher shift from their apartment to a more open and less crowded place in the outskirts of the city. It was a farm house of a friend which they took on rent. Slowly, they developed the idea of following a more natural and healthy way to live inspired by the village in which Aysher lived for a few months. Aysher knew all the sections of the village very well, so he tried to incorporate all the sections of the village into his house. With some changes, he revived the village which lived in his memories.

They bought a cow from which they got all the dairy products. Pottery was also included and this section became Risha's favourite. She used to spend hours making pots; they were just two people and didn't require so many pots. But she still used to make lots and then also paint them, after which she used to gift them to her friends.

Some friends used to visit Risha and Aysher at their farm house, which was vibrant and full of energy, and spend some quality time. They used to love spending time there. Aysher also became their family doctor, good health advisor, meditation instructor. Whenever there used to be holidays, lots of friends used to come over for days and spend some time with Aysher and Risha. Due to this, they made more huts with mud and bamboo. To make more huts, Aysher and Risha needed more land as the small farm was not enough to accommodate thirty to forty friends. So they sold their flat in the city and bought the nearby land, to accommodate small huts.

Their new small farm started as a place where Aysher and Risha could live a life similar to the life Aysher lived in the village, it soon became viral. Aysher's friend who had given his small farm on rent to him, asked him to accommodate his parents. In exchange, he donated the land to Aysher's NGO, 'Me Nature'. That was the name decided, and its aim was to live a life close to nature with simplicity.

When someone works for a good cause, lots of hands come and help, the same happened in this case. Lots of friends, societies, social workers, governments helped him financially to develop similar places.

Aysher's organization now covered the area of a village; it had a platform, huts, a cooking system, and various departments. It had lots and lots of greenery all around. There was solar electricity, and the communication was just via telephone and connection. He had some permanent residents, some came for wellness, on holidays and some for treatment. One thing was different from the village; each unit had a very rich library, and everyone was were encouraged to read.

Aysher was utilizing all his experiences and skills in one place, he and Risha lived amongst people who were like minded.

There was no competition around, there was no negativity, no anger. There was the fragrance of flowers, the flutter of birds, greenery of trees, fresh water and air, in which people lived and laughed freely.

Aysher's dream was slowly taking shape. Few of his friends and well-wishers, who were not living in the same city, wanted the same kind of infrastructure to be developed in their cities also. So, it was decided that Aysher would guide them and they would develop a similar place in their city, for the benefit of the society.

In three and a half years' time, Aysher's organization had developed eight villages on the outskirts of different cities, some were managed by his friends who felt the need for such spaces, they left their jobs to follow the leader. There was no shortage of funds or hands and with giant steps, Aysher's dream was taking shape.

The benefit that the residents were deriving from such a place, could not be expressed in words. With a healthy lifestyle, small health problems started to disappear and even serious diseases showed immense recovery.

But one thing was bothering Aysher. What he was doing was still limited. His wish was to include the whole human race into this type of living. He had a few ideas and he called for a meeting of all the people involved in the organization.

Chapter 23

❧

$\mathcal{I}$T WAS a bright sunny day when the meeting started under a huge banyan tree. Aysher stood in the middle and all his members sat in a circle. He started:

'Dear friends, your cooperation, love and support has brought all of us to this place.

I started this journey alone to get the answers to a lot of questions. I wandered, got lost in the woods, but found myself and also some ways, some rules, which is the only wealth I earned during my wandering.

My wanderings and the stories are known to all of you. We, as a family, have already started to live by the ways of the village. The village people were my guardians and parents whom I lost and now I live with the same values of love and friendship with my friends in a similar village. The soul of the village lives in my heart, and the villages that we have developed are different bodies of the same soul. I again thank you for the cooperation you have shown to fulfil my dream.

But there is one thing that disturbs my consciousness, friends. You people knew me earlier and showed faith in helping me, some even volunteered their services to help me. But what about those people who do not know any of us, how will they benefit? How can we help a man who goes for work in the morning and comes back home tired? How can we help the kids who are constantly engrossed in their studies? How can we help the patients who are being treated in hospitals? How can we help each and every person living on this planet earth, my friends?' The atmosphere totally changed to an emotional one, all his friends and well-wishers were very close to Aysher, and they were all waiting for his suggestions.

Aysher continued, 'We have to make everyone our member, and each member of ours would be taught certain ways of living a natural life. We will distribute saplings of herbs that can be used daily and would benefit the user. Certain booklets will be published and distributed, teaching each household the use of medicinal plants. Our organization will distribute paper and jute bags and spread awareness about the ill effects of plastic bags. Each member that we make, makes their way into our database. We will send them awareness tips, health care tips, home remedies and positive thoughts daily free of cost.' Risha was also listening attentively.

Aysher then suggested, 'We as a family want our family members to have a healthy body and mind. We also have to do a lot for global warming. Use of solar energy in vehicles is something we have to work on, and make it available for the people. We can easily use solar energy in street lights and solar lights-based home appliances.

And very importantly, we have to plant trees everywhere. We have to plant trees in our colonies, roadsides, cities, highways, even in barren lands and places where no one lives—on small islands, everywhere. Planting trees will increase the life of our planet. It is a solution for a lot of problems, like it will automatically reduce global warming, the water level is rising due to the melting of glaciers which will automatically get reduced, the erratic nature of the rainfall will become normal, which will benefit the farmers and majorly help in healing the ozone layer.'

After having a glass of water served by Risha, Aysher passionately said, 'We as a family will teach people how to live on the mother planet but in the healthiest way. We have to change our lifestyles. The way computers have crept into our lives, and have become a part of our lives, healthy lifestyle has to become a part of living. The plants and animals started their journey with us, but we have changed considerably. It's good, but now we have to change to improve our planet.

The targets are big and our hands are small, but my dear friends! If we work with dedication and towards the betterment of human race, God will definitely help us. This Earth is our mother and we are responsible for taking care of it.'

He looked at the people who were listening to him in zapped attention. He closed his eyes, thought about his Guru and mentally prayed for his support and guidance.

He was still standing when one of his friends, who was a doctor, came and hugged him. Aysher opened his eyes, saw his friend and hugged him with the same warmth. Slowly all his members were hugging him, he was standing in the centre and all his friends embraced the one ahead of him, to pledge for the cause.

Aysher worked without getting tired, the organization which worked for the benefit of the people had to expand its wings and help all. He sent proposals to organizations and governments, as to how they can work together for the well-being of the people.

More and more people started to get involved with the organization on a daily basis. All had various kinds of stories, so a special section was made that could maintain a database of all the people who were involved with the organization.

A special section was made that was involved with the scientific part of the organization. The NGO started to have units even in different countries.

Letters and e-mails poured in. First Aysher used to reply to them by himself, but when they increased and took up a lot of his time, Risha asked one of the members to type the replies while Aysher dictated. It was quite an interesting sight as Aysher used to walk all around doing his work and also dictating replies.

Risha was happy with this life. She knew what she meant for Aysher and she never asked him to marry her, or ask for any kind of a commitment. A look into each other's eyes was enough for both of them. She knew Aysher was passionate about helping all and she was happy helping him in such a great deed.

What made Aysher happy, was that he was working towards the wish of his Guruji and also that he was so important to so many people! Some called him son, some brother, and some friend. One day he was totally lost, and today he is guiding so many who are lost.

He was loving the change that had come about in his life. His hard work and of course the blessing of his Guru was taking him closer to his aim.

Chapter 24

AYSHER WAS sitting in his small mud hut and doing his paper work, it was the cold month of January. There was pin-drop silence, the cold had made everyone stay indoors. The air smelt of fog. The hut where Aysher was sitting was warm and cosy. He was slightly bent over his papers and was totally engrossed in his work. A little lamp was burning, and was kept close to the papers where he was working. The hut had a mattress in one corner and one more on which he was sitting. The other things in the room were a water container, and some books and files. It also included a small wooden table which was kept by the side of the bed. The table adorned a frame in which the letter written by Guruji was framed and in front of it, was the flower that was given to him by Hari; it had the same fragrance even after so many years. He was writing something, the flow of writing was still the same but the hands which wrote them, had lots of wrinkles on them.

It had been twenty-two years since Aysher started this organization and since then there was no looking back. He had completed his half century just a few days ago. The organization that he had started, had done the kind of work that no other place had done for the planet and its people. He had totally revolutionized the way people lived. He had not only preached, but had also made an effort to ensure that people can practice a new, simple yet healthy way to live, which was closer to nature.

There were some things that he had done that were big, and some were small, but each and every one had a strong effect and each worked for a better tomorrow.

The first thing that Aysher worked on, was to make people realize and believe that the simplest living was the best. He had already shifted from his posh flat to a farm, which gave him fresh air to breathe, farm fresh food to eat which he grew on his own, and he also made his body make some effort to earn his living. His requirements were simple two-time meals, a small place to sleep and planting trees as much as possible. This idea of his also got the support of his friends and well-wishers. There were some who came and started living along with him, some believed in Aysher's idea, some thought he was a recluse, some wanted to work towards Aysher's ideas. He found quite a number of people who joined him.

Aysher's friends who were in similar professional backgrounds in the media and multinational corporations, were the ones who provided him with a lot of backup. They were the ones who themselves could not join the organization as full time members, but they were the backbone to it. They had similar health issues and stress problems. Most of these people were the ones who took the organization and its deeds to the people—be it any country, each and every one was talking about it. It was a fragrance that charmed each human being.

We human beings know that certain things and some lifestyle is not good for the body, still we continue following it. Some lack the determination and some the time, so what

Aysher's organization did, was that they designed the website and network in such a manner that a person after selecting his profession and his location, could avail the ways in which he could follow ways that could help him in his well-being.

Aysher's organization was a hit with people who had serious ailments, and also with people with post-retirement stress. They left their homes to live a healthy and fulfilling life. Most cities had 'Camp Village' in their outskirts, the place was usually donated and the huts were made by simple mud with the effort of the people who later lived in them and called it their heaven. The food was grown by the people, cooked by the people. They planted trees in their surroundings, worked on all the aspects which Aysher learnt in 'his village'. They weaved, made pottery, took care of the animals for dairy products, some camps even did extensive work on locally available raw materials, like bamboo and wood. The camp villages had become places where people ultimately found solace after a long and tiring life.

The best thing that happened with this effort was that the camp villages helped the organization build a very good atmosphere. There were some people who were experts in their fields and post retirement, did not have much to do in life. They had seen life very closely, but this organization made them feel that there is more to their lives. It does not end at retirement or after making the kids independent, it's just the end of a phase.

These people were masters of different fields and now worked under the same roof, and towards the betterment of the society.

Aysher's organization grew in various countries. It was able to make people believe that the ones who reside in the normal villages can become a perfect example of a 'Camp Village' if they took into consideration some points. It was not that the villagers completely agreed to the ways of the organization, but they slowly understood and tried to make a few changes. The best part was that the villagers gained the confidence that they are in no way lacking, but they were the ones with a better lifestyle.

The plantation drive of the organization had touched the heart of the people because it had the maximum followers. Followers were not one-click followers, but people who sweated in the sun, made efforts and reached places to plant trees. This step drastically changed the planet. Now global warming was history, earthquakes, irregular rains, floods, seasonal changes—all natural environmental irregularities were in place again. Because of this, each crop had a massive yield, food items became cheaper and the air became clean.

Many offices did something very unusual, the idea given by one of Aysher's camp village residents. He suggested that people should go to office only for a day in the week and the rest of the work they should do online. This idea was initially questioned a lot, but later it became viral. The people who worked from home did not require to travel, which meant that pollution was lessened, less social stress and more time was given to the family and its welfare. Health also started to improve.

This brought one more change—the children also got more attention at home. And so schools also started to operate on the internet. The studies were online, same as the exams. The mental health of the people of the world started to improve with these efforts. The kids got more attention from the parents and so their grades also improved. Study was made more interactive and vast. Due to the availability of the internet, kids were also learning new and innovative things specially designed by Aysher's organization.

Daily there was some new information by Aysher's NGO on the blog including articles by engineers, scientists, psychologists, therapists, doctors, nutritionists, environmentalist, and teachers. The buildings which had earlier held space for schools and offices, were now either camp villages or gardens with lots of plants, trees and animals.

Aysher was the most sought-after person of the world, yet the popularity had brought no change in him. He was still working with the same zeal for the betterment of the human race, each day non-stop.

His latest achievement was a report from the UN that the ozone layer had recovered fifty per cent in comparison to its earlier condition, due to the efforts of Aysher's organization and its work on the environment. This was a big reason for the members of the organization to rejoice. According to the report, Earth was healing itself.

The door of Aysher's hut opened and Risha came in; it was her usual routine to bring the morning milk, and turmeric milk at night for Aysher. He was working on his papers. He knew and didn't needed to lift up his face to recognize her.

Sometimes we ask very little from life when it is ready to give us its best. Risha wanted a husband and wife relationship for them, she did not get that as they never got married. But what she got from life, was a true union from his soul. She knew in this life or in any other, she and he would always be together till eternity. She was a part of his soul and vice versa. And such a relationship needed no certificate. They were two yet one, till they adopted a girl child who Risha found near the garbage dump—the baby was hurt and she was the one who rescued the screeching baby from a dog. As soon as she picked up the baby, it clutched on to her clothes and did not let her go for a whole day. A bond was created, she knew what she had to do. As the medical treatment of the baby was being done, it came to light that the baby was dumped not because she was a girl but because she had a disease. After completing all the formalities, Risha became the proud mother of a perfect human being, she was now healthy and was about to celebrate her seventeenth birthday. They named her 'Prakriti'. Prakriti called Aysher 'baba' and they also shared a perfect bond. Although Aysher's organization had rescued many orphans with similar or different situations, but Prakriti was lucky as she was the legal daughter of Risha, and Aysher was her Godfather.

Risha entered and kept the milk in one corner, she then tidied his bed, collected all the papers and sat beside him waiting for him to complete his work and to share the most precious time of the day.

It was after fifteen to twenty minutes that Aysher lifted his head and smiled naughtily, 'You... you still make me wait... that's not fair.' She said complaining. 'That's my favourite hobby, dear and I thoroughly enjoy it,' replied Aysher, and they both started laughing.

'It's cold outside and you have a tiring day ahead, I will advise you to sleep and finish this work later,' she said with concern.

Aysher lifted his head, looked at Risha, she looked concerned and he closed his eyes. Risha again said, 'The helicopter will be here to take you to the ceremony by 8:30 a.m. All the preparations are complete. I am so happy and proud of you. Tomorrow, you will be rewarded for your efforts, your hard work.'

Aysher was listening to all this with closed eyes, he opened them after some time and looked at Risha. 'What is the matter Aysher? You don't seem relaxed,' she asked as she held his hand.

Aysher closed his file and after stretching his hands said, 'You know the reason Risha, I have never approved of these awards. I don't want them, how can they award a person who is a seeker; I am still a seeker. I don't want all the name and fame it will bring along. I don't want awards, I want something else...but...'

'But!' interrupted Risha... 'Some things are done for the wish of others...the people of the organization are so happy... they are feeling as if they are being give this award. Do you realize it is the biggest award in the history of mankind. All the countries of the whole world have signed for this award. It is unique, and it has the blessings of so many human beings. There is nothing bigger than this. I agree that there is more to life, but as a human being nothing can beat this. I don't believe this...at least respect the feelings of others...do you realize what you have done...you have changed the ways of living of the whole human race. Earlier they were building houses of stones and bricks and were trying to secure themselves from the others and you have made them break those barriers to live like a huge, huge family which has lakhs and lakhs of members. I agree there are still some who do not agree with your ways. But there is a larger number who follow you. They love you for what you have done, they think that you have done the greatest job ever. You have changed the living patterns of the humans. Earlier there was bloodshed, everyone was fighting for their space. Now people know the meaning of love and sharing. Isn't this big?' she questioned.

Aysher looked at her and calmly said, 'You are right, it is big but if it is big, as you say it is, why do I still fell restless? There is still something pushing me. I feel I still have more to do. Why?'

Risha came closer and said in a softer voice 'Aysher, you will feel that drive, because that drive is the one which had brought you this far. See, you have made such lovely 'Camp Villages', they have all the facilities one can think of; solar lights, fresh air, all sorts of animals, birds, cows, ducks, dogs all live in them. There are ponds in them for the use of water, no plastic is used in them, and they grow their own crops and consume it. They teach kids, they are scientifically very developed. Regularly some new eco-friendly gadget is developed.'

'Your work is not restricted to the 'Camp Villages', you have bought lands for the organization and dug up so many water reservoirs for water harvesting. You have distributed some basic medicinal saplings free of cost in the cities and even informed people about their uses. People are aware about the environment now. The environment has improved drastically, now the number of fatal diseases has also decreased. And not to forget, the recycling of garbage has created new fertilisers, now most of the houses also make fertilizers which we buy, and distribute to the farmers free of cost. This idea was also a hit.

Ratio of poor people have also come down as crops have such high yields and food is available at a lower cost now.

And the scientists of our organization have worked so much on the idea to grow trees even in remote places, by the use of drones. The glaciers have stopped melting now, do you want God to come and say to you that you have done something g-r-e-a-t-?'

She then paused, 'Be humble Aysher, respect your work and

the feeling of others. Sleep early and get up quickly. Prakriti has a surprise for you, she will give it to you in the morning.' She then again paused and saw Aysher smiling.

'Why? What happened? I will not stop lecturing you, no matter how old I get,' said Risha. And they both started to laugh again.

The beauty of their relationship, was that nothing could separate them from each other, not even they themselves. They talked for some time and then Risha left. She knew exactly what Aysher was talking about, but she didn't want to discuss it. There was a big day waiting for him and she wanted to make him happy and think of his achievements rather than repenting what he hasn't got.

Thoughtfully, she walked towards her hut and found Prakriti awake, still waiting for her mother.

There was just the sound of the wind that could be heard in the cold night. Risha walked towards her hut where the lamp was still flickering, she had two pillars in her life—one was Aysher and another was Prakriti. She opened the door only to find Prakriti all curled up in her blanket, her curly hair were cascading down the sides of her face, her eyes were fish like, her nose was pointed and lips were like the petals of pink roses. She was a true replica of her name 'Prakriti'. She had really grown up to her name, the Mother Goddess.

'Ma! Where were you? I was waiting for you...the project you have given me, has brought some questions to my mind,' said Prakriti, complaining.

'I had just gone to visit Baba and remind him of tomorrow's schedule. You know he does not like to be in the limelight,' replied Risha.

'Hmm, I agree…' she said nodding. 'Come here, Ma…let me show you my work,' and she shifted a little to make space for her mother.

Risha thoroughly enjoyed her motherhood, she had no complaints from life and felt complete. She went and joined her daughter in the warm and cosy blanket. 'Ooooo Ma, your feet are so cold! First you have your milk, you will feel better,' and she picked up the cup and handed it to her mother.

'Ma, look. What do you think of these sites for setting up a camp village near Pithoragarh?' she questioned still looking closely at the pictures on her laptop. She waited for some time for the response and then again questioned her mother. Risha was still thinking about Aysher.

'Ma, Ma where are you? Look here. I need your advice. I am utterly confused,' said Prakriti.

Risha quickly winded up her thoughts and looked towards her darling daughter. She then held her face in both her hands and looking deep into her eyes and said, 'I love you, and have full faith in your goodness. This goodness will always help and guide you. Be patient. The Almighty will always be by your side.'

'That is perfectly fine. I know things will always be good for me, but Ma, why don't you or Baba come along with me just for a day and help me choose a proper location. See, you both have a lot of experience, why cannot I get some benefit out of it? Maaa…' said Prakriti moving her head.

'Why don't you tie your hair, they become so unmanageable sometimes. Get some oil, I will apply some oil to your hair,' said Risha.

Prakriti got up and got the bottle of mustard oil and a comb and sat in front of her mother. Risha oiled her hair and tied them into a plait.

She then beckoned her daughter to come and sit by her side and said, 'To be honest, Baba does not want to go to the place where he had lost his loving village, it was an immense loss of his life, and he does not want to revive its memories. I personally do not want to go there because I lost your Baba there. I have also some very sad experience from that place.'

'But life has moved on Ma....you and Baba are together now.'

'Yes we are together, but there are some chapters in life which one does not want to relive. Going there will revive it all. That place is all new for you. It has a whole lot of opportunities. Hills might show you a completely new direction. I will also let you know the exact location of the Baba's lost village. You might find something which you will want to share with Baba. Maybe some villagers might have been saved in the tragedy and now have rebuilt the village. Maybe you will be able to find some remains of that temple.' There were twinkles of hope in Risha and Prakriti's eyes.

'Baba has given you a great responsibility, you have worked with us very closely on many projects and you know the nitty-gritties of the camp villages. You have a huge responsibility on your young shoulders. We have a lot of expectations from you, maybe you can take on the project with your new ideas and hard work,' said the emotional Risha.

'OK, Ma. You are absolutely right. But just one more question, what is the most difficult part of the Camp Village?' questioned Prakriti.

'That's a tough one but the most difficult part of a camp village and life is, to win hearts. I hope you win more than your Baba,' answered Risha.

'Come on, it's late and I have to get up very early as Baba has to go for the award.'

'Baba does not seem excited! Isn't it a great achievement for him?' questioned the curious Prakriti.

'Yes it is a great achievement, but that was not he wanted in life,' she explained while adjusting the bed.

'I got you, Ma, I know you are a genius in explaining things, how have you mastered this art?' They both giggled and cuddled in the warm blanket.

Risha was about to sleep when suddenly Prakriti again came up with another question.

'Will you both never go again to that hill, not even to see my Camp Village?'

Risha knew the answer but it was difficult to explain to the young heart. She preferred to keep silent.

Chapter 25

*A*YSHER WAS sitting alone in his hut, there was pin-drop silence around. If one goes by the atmosphere around, there should be peace and calmness inside him but inside, he felt the opposite. His heart was pumping as if he was running a race. His restlessness was increasing every minute. His breathing became heavy, which made him shut all the work he was doing. He got up and tried to have a glass of water, the gulping process of a water never seemed so difficult for him. He was feeling giddy and had a severe headache at the same time.

The sudden change in his health made him difficult to understand the reason for such a situation. Of whatever he could understand, he analysed that he was not happy with the prize which he was being felicitated with. It was indeed, the highest award that a human being could receive. It was a joint effort of all the countries to thank him for his great contribution to save the environment. He felt as if the prize was being tied around his neck and as if he was not the deserving person for the award. His uneasiness was not reducing, it even scared him a little. First, he thought of calling out for some help, but then he thought that it's better to be alone even if these are the last few moments of his life, and it was unworthy to disturb the ones who are resting.

He then took a few steps and struggled to open the door. As soon as the door opened, he saw a tall, well-built figure standing in front of him. He could hardly see the face but the positive aura could be felt. He bent at the feet of the figure and curled around them. Tears of joy started to drop from his eyes; he was overwhelmed. Life for him came to a standstill. A few moments ago, he was feeling as if these were the last few moments of his life and now after a few seconds, he was curling around his anchor.

There was a pause, a long pause, even the breeze stopped to see the meeting of the two ends. Student and teacher were the two ends, each is complete when it meets the other. Aysher's health improved as soon as touched the pious feet, and even the saintly figure felt a lot of relief after touching the plant nurtured by him.

After some time Aysher said, 'Guruji, you took quite long to come, a delay of a few seconds and I would have left this world.'

Guruji, held Aysher by his shoulders and made him stand. It was the first time, he was face to face with his mentor and guide. Guruji looked younger than Aysher, he was well built. His hair reached his shoulder. His eyes were big and black in colour. His nose was sharp. His lips were dark and his smile was more beautiful than anything else in this world. He looked at Aysher with caring eyes, stroked a hand on his head and hugged him tightly.

'I knew this was coming, son. I could feel your uneasiness, I was always with you, and you have done a great job. I am proud of you, son and also that you are my student.' All these words were as if falling on deaf ears because Aysher was clinging to

Guruji and felt as if he had touched the most pure and coolest thing of the world.

Guruji and Aysher kept on standing at the doorway for some time, it was only later that Aysher got his senses back and realized that he was still clinging to Guruji. And that he should stop behaving in such a kiddish manner. It is always difficult let go a thing so pious, and they both stepped inside the hut.

Indeed the hut felt blessed to witness such a historic event.

As Guruji stepped in, Aysher guided him towards his bedding and for himself, he chose to sit on the floor near the sacred feet of his lord. Tears were continuously flowing from Aysher' eyes, he tried many times but was unable to control them. Guruji closely observed the hut in all the directions and Aysher's eyes were transfixed only on his guide.

Life had come around a full circle for him, there was a day he started his journey with the inspiration from his guru, and when the journey reached its culminating point, the inspiration was sitting in front of him. This can be now taken as an achievement.

Aysher was lost in his own thoughts when Guruji asked him, 'Your room looks so perfect Aysher! But tell me when will you leave this tendency of giving up on your life. If I am right, this was the fourth effort?'

Aysher lowered his head, and said in a very slow voice, 'When you are around, then.'

'But I am always with you, each time you are in need, I am the one who comes to your rescue. Maybe that is the reason you reach such stages. Why do you want to punish yourself? You are such a beautiful creation of the Almighty, I am your guide, what is that you have deep inside your heart that bothers you?' he asked Aysher.

'Guruji!,' he said just that and paused. He was scared to utter out such words from his mouth.

Guruji understood his situation and said, 'This is for your own good Aysher. If you want to be empty from within, let all the thoughts, negative and positive, pass through your soul. Don't ever let any thought stay there. It will occupy space and be like a magnet to the other thoughts. Let things pass, let time pass, let people play their role in life and pass by, let thoughts pass, just hold on to your inner soul. The soul which was always there, which will always be, it has no end nor any start; it is the one that is there, or rather it is the only one that is true, rest is nothing.'

Aysher still sat near the feet of his guide. He collected all his courage to speak and then in a very soft voice he said, 'Guruji, I have a very heavy burden over my shoulders, I am carrying it since such a long time, please free me from this.' He then paused and then again continued, 'I have the burden of hundreds of death, and I am the cause. I have betrayed the faith of those who nurtured me in my bad times. I am a culprit. They took care of me as their own and I betrayed them. Vaidji, who was my friend and guide had warned me earlier only that if I leave the Sacred Forest before fifty-one days, a bad omen will come to the village. His saying to me seemed real and I believed him, but the day I started to think of my own benefit, I simply forgot what he said. I am the reason because of which the village got washed away in the floods. Please save me from this sin that I have committed, I cannot bear it anymore,' and he started to cry bitterly.

Guruji leaned a bit forward and caressed Aysher's head, 'Son, look at me', he called again and Aysher lifted his red eyes. 'Son, you have learnt a lot, served the human race to the fullest, but you are still in need of teaching. You still have not moved away from the feeling of 'the doer'', he said.

Aysher soon stopped crying and listened carefully. 'Aysher, do you really think you are the doer?' he waited for his Guru to utter the golden words.

'These words are not for you only, these words are for all the living creatures, the humans, the trees, the animals, the water, the air, the planets, the soil, everything.

'You are not the doer, you don't do any action, all actions are done because He wants you to do them, and you are just a medium. Why do you think that you are the reason for the destruction of the village? Then why do you think you went to the village? He took you to the village, and made you experience everything. He made you feel restless in such a pious village. You reached the cave, then you wanted to run from there also. You brought about such a drastic change in the world. He wanted the change! So you were the medium, through you He achieved it. Like, you were saved from death a number of times, who saved you? Not me, nor the villagers, He saved you. All that happens, happens because, He wants them to happen,' said Guruji.

Now Aysher was listening as if his whole body had become just ears, all his pores, all his hair, all his organs had become ears. He was listening.

Guruji then stood up, his white clothes were dazzling in the faint light of the lamp as if, diamonds were hidden inside his shawl. Aysher kept sitting, and listening.

He again said, 'There is one more thing, even more important than the previous. Why do you think that you and I are different? We are all one, you and the person sitting kilometres away from you, who doesn't even know you, you both are the same. You and the bird are the same, we are all part of the same. There is nothing beyond that 'One'. It is only that which is present, all that your eyes see, is all virtual. You, me, this hut, this flower, this glass of milk, the moon, the trees, the breeze that flows, the sky, all the humans of the planet, the galaxies, all are part of the One. The day the human race sees above the feeling of you and me, that day will be the day of salvation for all. So, develop love for all.'

He then extended his hand towards Aysher and said, 'Bless you my son, may you find Him within,' saying this Guruji turned, he took a few steps and opened the door. Aysher kept on sitting in his place just like a statue. His eyes were closed, only his ears were listening. Soon he realized the sound of the wind had increased and also the footsteps of someone walking briskly could be heard. He opened his eyes, there was no one in the room. The door was open and strong wind was flowing, Aysher shouted, 'Guruji!' and ran outside.

Guruji was a brisk walker, he had come halfway through the Camp Village, he heard the footsteps of someone but he did not stop. Aysher also saw Guruji from a distance, he started to run hysterically as if running for his life. The shawl from Aysher's shoulder fell. He came running to where Guruji was, and held his feet from behind. 'I beg your guidance, Guruji please don't leave me now, I have waited for you for long. Now, I want to live with you, I don't want to live a life which is void of you. For me, you are my life and I will not let you go,' said Aysher.

Guruji helped him get up, and smiled at his child, 'I love all my children but I love the ones a little more who live in the hearts of many. You are loved by many Aysher. Come we have somewhere to go.'

And both the figures walked away.

It was very early in the morning that Risha stepped out of her hut, it was her daily routine to get up early and go and meet Aysher. As she walked toward Aysher's hut, she felt something different in the air, as if something was about to take her by surprise. She quickened her steps a little, at a distance of a few steps, she saw something lying on the floor, she hastened a little more and as she reached closer, she saw Aysher's shawl lying in the mud. As she picked it up, she got a little scared, and ran towards his hut.

As she reached, she saw the door of the hut open and Aysher was nowhere to be seen. 'Aysher! Aysher!' she shouted many times but there was no reply. But there was a different smell in the hut, being a sensitive person she could feel the difference. Tears ran down her eyes. She held the shawl close to her heart and ran outside, shouting his name. While running, she noticed some footprints, earlier there were two footprints which were at a different pace from each other, after some distance she saw a little patch of mud where she noticed two footprints and one footprint of someone sitting. As she saw this, a faint smile came over her face and also tears started to trickle down her eyes. She sat there and understood the whole story. She was happy and also sad at the same time. She was happy for Aysher, as he had met his Guru. And on the other hand, she was sad that she had lost her love.

She touched the pure mud where once Guruji stood. She could clearly see four footprints moving at the same pace after that patch. She slowly got up and tried to follow but after some distance, the footprints became blurred. She returned to Aysher's hut sobbing for her loss.

As she sat on the bed, she saw that Aysher had not finished his turmeric milk at night. She tried to control her tears, looked up at the ceiling of the hut, and felt sorry for herself as she was left alone to tread the path of life.

As she moved her eyes around the hut in a hope to see the same face again, something caught her attention.

She left the shawl on the bedding and stepped forward. What she saw amazed her. There was a letter with her name on it.

Dear Risha,

When you will find this letter, I will be gone. Last night, Guruji came and I now want to go along with him. I think you and I both knew that this was about to come. We together did a lot of things, now, I think, it is time for us to take separate paths.

I always wanted to be with my Guru and here I am. I am happy and content. I will always pray for you and hope you find happiness. I have nothing to offer as I myself am a beggar. I just have my prayers and also hope you will take over my responsibilities.

I thank you for being there with me in all the phases of my life. I hope you will pardon me as I am going again, leaving you alone.

Life is uncertain Risha. I hope our paths cross soon. Wishing you all the love.

Do take care of Prakriti and tell her Baba loves her. She will always be in my prayers. I know she will make us proud.

Hope you find your anchor as I have found mine.

Blessings,
Aysher.

Risha finished the letter and started to cry, but someone held her from behind, lovingly. It was Prakriti.

Aysher handed over all his achievements and again became empty, an empty space that was ready to be filled again. Later the award that Aysher had to receive was collected by Risha on his behalf.

The place where Risha had found Guruji's foot marks, a marble stone was installed there. The award was also kept there as it belonged to the society. That place was proof that the true seeker always finds whatever he wants. And, also, that the seeker can never find his guide only the guide can find his student.

Life at all stages tells us that there is always SOMEWHERE TO GO...

Acknowledgements

This book has been a wonderful journey for me as an author to reach my soul, and that journey is only possible when you have the blessings of God.

It is a privilege to be born and later get married into a family of achievers where everyone is supportive and loving. I thank my friends who have always been so encouraging.

I also thank my readers and hope my writing was able to touch their lives in some way.

Finally, I would like to thank Rupa Publications who have made the publishing of my novel a piece of cake. I am lucky to have met good people always!